THE
JOURNEY
PRIZE

STORIES

WINNERS OF THE $10,000 JOURNEY PRIZE

1989: Holley Rubinsky for "Rapid Transits"

1990: Cynthia Flood for "My Father Took a Cake to France"

1991: Yann Martel for "The Facts Behind the Helsinki Roccamatios"

1992: Rozena Maart for "No Rosa, No District Six"

1993: Gayla Reid for "Sister Doyle's Men"

1994: Melissa Hardy for "Long Man the River"

1995: Kathryn Woodward for "Of Marranos and Gilded Angels"

1996: Elyse Gasco for "Can You Wave Bye Bye, Baby?"

1997 (shared): Gabriella Goliger for "Maladies of the Inner Ear"
                    Anne Simpson for "Dreaming Snow"

1998: John Brooke for "The Finer Points of Apples"

1999: Alissa York for "The Back of the Bear's Mouth"

2000: Timothy Taylor for "Doves of Townsend"

2001: Kevin Armstrong for "The Cane Field"

2002: Jocelyn Brown for "Miss Canada"

2003: Jessica Grant for "My Husband's Jump"

2004: Devin Krukoff for "The Last Spark"

2005: Matt Shaw for "Matchbook for a Mother's Hair"

2006: Heather Birrell for "BriannaSusannaAlana"

2007: Craig Boyko for "OZY"

2008: Saleema Nawaz for "My Three Girls"

2009: Yasuko Thanh for "Floating Like the Dead"

2010: Devon Code for "Uncle Oscar"

2011: Miranda Hill for "Petitions to Saint Chronic"

2012: Alex Pugsley for "Crisis on Earth-X"

2013: Naben Ruthnum for "Cinema Rex"

2014: Tyler Keevil for "Sealskin"

2015: Deirdre Dore for "The Wise Baby"

2016: Colette Langlois for "The Emigrants"

2017: Sharon Bala for "Butter Tea at Starbucks"

The BEST of CANADA'S NEW WRITERS

THE JOURNEY PRIZE

STORIES

SELECTED BY

SHARON BALA
KERRY CLARE
ZOEY LEIGH PETERSON

McCLELLAND & STEWART

Library and Archives Canada Cataloguing in Publication is available upon
request

The lines on p. 120 are from *The Tale of Kieu* by Nguyen Du, as translated by
Cam-Loi Huynh.

The epigraph to "Never Prosper" is from the piece "Nervous Splendor" by
Anthony Gottlieb, published in the April 9 issue of *The New Yorker*.

Published simultaneously in the United States of America by McClelland &
Stewart, a Penguin Random House Company

Library of Congress Control Number is available upon request

ISBN: 978-0-7710-5075-6
ebook ISBN: 978-0-7710-5076-3

Typeset in Janson by M&S, Toronto
Printed and bound in Canada

McClelland & Stewart,
a division of Penguin Random House Canada Limited,
a Penguin Random House Company
www.penguinrandomhouse.ca

1 2 3 4 5   22 21 20 19 18

Penguin
Random House
McCLELLAND & STEWART

ABOUT THE JOURNEY PRIZE STORIES

The $10,000 Journey Prize is awarded annually to an emerging writer of distinction. This award, now in its thirtieth year, and given for the eighteenth time in association with the Writers' Trust of Canada as the Writers' Trust of Canada/ McClelland & Stewart Journey Prize, is made possible by James A. Michener's generous donation of his Canadian royalty earnings from his novel *Journey*, published by McClelland & Stewart in 1988. The Journey Prize itself is the most significant monetary award given in Canada to a developing writer for a short story or excerpt from a fiction work in progress. The winner of this year's Journey Prize will be selected from among the thirteen stories in this book.

The Journey Prize Stories has established itself as the most prestigious annual fiction anthology in the country, introducing readers to the finest new literary writers from coast to coast for three decades. It has become a who's who of up-and-coming writers, and many of the authors who have appeared in the anthology's pages have gone on to distinguish themselves with short story collections, novels, and literary awards. The anthology comprises a selection from submissions made by the editors of literary journals and annual anthologies from across the country, who have chosen what, in their view, is the most exciting writing in English that they have published in the previous year. In recognition of the vital role journals play in fostering literary voices, McClelland & Stewart makes its own award of $2,000 to the journal or anthology that originally published and submitted the winning entry.

This year the selection jury comprised three acclaimed writers:

Sharon Bala lives in St. John's, where she is a member of The Port Authority writing group. In 2017, two of her short stories were included in *The Journey Prize Stories 29*, and her story "Butter Tea at Starbucks" went on to win the Writers' Trust / McClelland & Stewart Journey Prize. Her debut novel, *The Boat People*, was a #1 national bestseller and was a finalist for CBC's Canada Reads and the Amazon Canada First Novel Award. Please visit SharonBala.com.

Kerry Clare is a National Magazine Award-nominated writer, editor of *The M Word: Conversations About Motherhood*, and author of the novel *Mitzi Bytes*. She is the editor of the Canadian books website 49thShelf.com, and has been writing about books and reading on her blog, Pickle Me This, for more than a decade.

Zoey Leigh Peterson was born in England, grew up in the United States, and has spent most of her adult life in Canada. Her fiction has appeared in *The Walrus*, *EVENT*, *Grain*, *PRISM international*, and has been anthologized in *The Journey Prize Stories* and *Best Canadian Stories*. She is the recipient of the Far Horizons Award for Short Fiction and the Peter Hinchcliffe Fiction Award. Her debut novel, *Next Year, For Sure*, was longlisted for the 2017 Scotiabank Giller Prize and shortlisted for the BC Book Prize's Ethel Wilson Fiction Prize and a Lambda Literary Award.

The jury read a total of one hundred submissions without knowing the names of the authors or those of the publications in which the stories originally appeared. McClelland & Stewart would like to thank the jury for their efforts in selecting this year's anthology and, ultimately, the winner of this year's Journey Prize.

McClelland & Stewart would also like to acknowledge the continuing enthusiastic support of writers, literary editors, and the public in the common celebration of new voices in Canadian fiction.

For more information about *The Journey Prize Stories*, please visit www.facebook.com/TheJourneyPrize.

CONTENTS

INTRODUCTION

A package arrived in the mail. Inside: exactly one hundred short stories with the authors' names blacked out. Our job was to read them all and choose the very best for inclusion in the thirtieth edition of *The Journey Prize Stories*. The instructions were straightforward. The decisions were not.

One hundred disparate works of art, each a unique specimen with its own plot, characters, and style. What does it mean to be "the best"? Does it mean the most accomplished? The most original? The most ambitious? The most important or timely?

One requirement that was immediately obvious: the narrative of the story had to pull us in and keep us asking, "What happens next?" Crisp prose was desirable, of course, and deep emotion very welcome. But first and foremost, a story had to excite our curiosity and grip it to the end.

It also had to show us something new and, paradoxically, something old, something we recognized from the world. The stories that delighted us were ones that recast the familiar— stories that took an emotion, place, or theme we knew well and turned it to show us a new angle. Regina through the eyes of a student from Uganda; a mercurial friendship between two older women; being lost in the woods inside a bear that isn't a bear; a story that name drops Cheever in the first paragraph, then veers in a direction Cheever would never have gone.

To be clear: we three jurors did not always see eye to eye, at least not on the first read. However, as we debated and reconsidered, our opinions shifted and coalesced. Unsurprisingly, the stories that emerged as our unanimous selections were ones that reward re-examination—tales so rich they reveal new insights on second, third, and even fourth reads.

This process of discussing and engaging and, ultimately, selecting has made us increasingly thoughtful and critical readers. As we whittled down the selections, we were forced to interrogate not just the stories, but also our own aesthetic preferences and biases. The thirteen that remain came through this crucible unscathed.

In this collection, you will find stories set in Vietnam and Spain and California, in a suburban strip mall in the Prairies, and at track level in a Toronto subway station. Some are minimalist, spare in detail but rich in emotional truth. Others are densely written, full of startling metaphor and image. There is birth. There is death. Also: love triangles, parental anxiety, betrayal, grief, adventure, unexpected moments of levity, and arresting dialogue. All are thoughtful explorations of what it means to be alive, rendered with inquisitiveness, insight, and uncertainty.

Yes, these stories are suspended in uncertainty—about what, exactly, has happened; about whose point of view is reliable; about what conclusions we might draw at a story's end. At times, this can be unsettling for the characters and readers alike. But these thirteen stories also underline the expansive potential of uncertainty, which requires one to reach beyond the limits of their knowledge, and demands an openness to asking questions, considering different answers, and finding new possibilities in mutability.

For the past three decades, the Journey Prize anthology has been a harbinger, a sampling of the literary talent emerging in this country. This year in particular, as Canadian literature struggles to dismantle what is broken and rebuild a better, stronger culture from within, it is heartening to read the stories in this collection, each one meticulously crafted and told with precision and care. These stories and their authors, with their assured new voices, represent the future of literature in this country. And the future is hopeful.

Sharon Bala
Kerry Clare
Zoey Leigh Peterson
May 2018

AVIVA DALE MARTIN

BARCELONA

You call and tell me you have a flat in Barcelona for the month of August. In September you will be renting a car to drive to France.

Join me in Spain. Join me in France.

I was hoping to stay home and swim at the beach this newly retired summer. And paint a large canvas in my backyard.

But

Free lodging. Sharing car expenses.

You can't miss this opportunity, you tell me.

I can't.

While I try to salvage something of my summer plans, you go ahead of me. I swim every day in cool Pacific waters but never get to the canvas. Instead there is organizing and arranging and packing to do.

You meet me at Plaza Sant Jaume after you have waited in midday heat for two hours. You lead me to our flat. My jetlagged mind flickers with images of stone walls and window pots. My suitcase rolls and jumps behind me, sending messages from antiquity through my body. Time travel.

We have walked to Barcelona's nude beach. We place our sarongs on the sand amid swimmers and sunbathers who wear bottoms or bikinis or nothing at all. You wear nothing at all. You are tall and slim and your wispy, layered blond hair sweeps your face. One of your nipples has a bright pinkish scar beneath it from the lumpectomy you had in the spring. Even naked you stand with poise, graceful. Even naked at seventy-two, you are elegant.

I want to hide in my clothes. But I take them off to reveal sagging skin and breasts that drop to my waist. A pronounced curve in my spine raises one hip almost an inch above the other. Exposed, I walk to the water's edge. And enter. The warm Mediterranean Sea is my sanctuary.

You were so happy to see me. You'd put food in the fridge: oranges, cheeses, bread, wine. You'd spent days washing the floors, my bedding, making a place for my stuff. You squeezed orange juice for my breakfast.

We sit at the table mornings and evenings and talk for hours. You tell me about your previous travels in Spain and Italy and Turkey. And stories from your three weeks here before I arrived. You show me the blouse you bought at the Miró museum and the silk scarves from the Picasso. You read to me from the travel books you have carted with you.

The route from my room to the toilet takes me past your bed but you are a light sleeper and you do not want me to leave my room. You hand me a yellow bucket to pee into. At four in the morning, I am still awake with jetlag and the eight-hour time change and the bucket is almost full. I take a sleeping pill.

You are so eager to show me the Barcelona you have discovered. Everything is new and rich to me. Everything is old and familiar to you. You lead me along your preferred routes, pointing out things you love: your favourite cafe, the enormous Lichtenstein sculpture on our way to the beach, the outdoor market where you bought your sarong. As we walk you tell me more stories of your adventures here and point to what I should notice. I look past your stories to the flower boxes and floating curtains that decorate windows. I finger the ancient stones in the high wall bordering the courtyard at the end of our street, stopping to follow cracks and mortar, up, up, with my eyes.

Your voice surrounds me like gauze, separating me from my journey. You are telling me about the kitten that lives down that street. Let's go that way to find it. Your words pull me away from the cathedral at the end of the block. We stop for you to caress every animal we meet. You have long talks with the dogs and their owners while I try to break away, to find my own experience. When we locate the cat, you grin up at me seeking my collusion. I watch you caress the animal, silent about my aversion to pets.

My arm is sore from trying to unlock the door to our apartment. You have tried to teach me how: push the key in, turn it, pull it halfway back, turn it the rest of the way while pushing the door with the other hand. You are not impatient, assuring me that it took you days to get it. We mount the sixty-four breathless stairs and I sink when you hand me the key to attempt it again. I know it won't work but if I say that you'll blame my negative thoughts for my failure.

Because I can't open the door to our apartment I have to stay with you when we go out. I have to listen to your continuous stories, your impressions that block out my own. Your favourite routes are not the shortest. You want to walk and walk and walk, and I follow, my back sore. You show concern for my back pain but continue to lead me on the longest course. I want to stop and rest and see the street musicians, Spanish guitar, flamenco. You stop with me but you talk and talk and talk.

We finish our novels at almost the same time and exchange them, both books by Canadian women authors, both of us preferring print on paper to e-books. After you have read the first chapter of Lisa Moore's *February* you tell me that two of your favourite sections were ones I'd underlined. At the back of *Lullabies for Little Criminals*, I find you've made notes of the same pages and paragraphs I intend to reread. We are drunk with the two authors' stunning imagery and we laugh and hug to find our reading preferences and styles so similar.

We decide to extend our wardrobes by sharing and hang our clothes together. You are generous, encouraging me to wear your expensive, classy outfits. You fix up my hair and lend me your jewellery. We pose like models, with sucked-in cheeks, in front of the pockmarked mirror.

You tell me that my hot flashes, which have tormented me for ten years, sweat pouring out of my body to drench my pillow and derange my sleep, should be viewed differently, as an opportunity, a gift, that they allow me to detoxify. My own portable sauna. No more complaining! But I can't stop my urgent seeking of shadows when a hot flash begins under a malicious sun.

My niece Gracie asked me how well we knew each other when I told her of these travel plans. I told her how we had met two years ago in Mexico. Two women travelling alone. Five days of swimming, five nights of dancing. It felt like a romance: exciting, joyful, so much in common. We returned home and kept in touch. When you invited me to join you on this trip I hadn't thought to be cautious of strangers.

In late August, Barcelona nights in the Barri Gotic are a gentle, sleeveless warmth. The buskers are at every plaza, flamenco guitar, cello, opera, even Shakespeare. Sometimes you are quiet when they play. We stroll and stop and unload our pockets of the coins we've saved for these virtuosos.

We stop for coffee in the morning, wine at night. You show me pictures of your lover and tell me of his attentions in rich detail. You want me to agree that he looks good. You read me his emails and commandeer me to help you select a fitting gift for him. We go into bookstores and shoe stores. You buy something but change your mind and return it the next day. I want to show you pictures of my daughter and my grandchildren. You glance, then look away. Narcissistic, I think.

We go to bed before midnight, pulling ourselves away from the intense talk we share at our kitchen table when we return each night. We have a routine to keep me from walking past your bed in the nook between my room and the bathroom and kitchen. I gather everything I might need: water, a midnight snack, my reading glasses, my iPad. I have my last toilet pee, we hug goodnight, and I walk through the long, windowed hallway to my little windowless bedroom at the end. You have asked me to keep the hallway windows closed because of the street noises, neighbours talking till five in the morning, restaurants moving tables inside at two or three a.m. It is very stuffy in this room where I spend my nights and very hot in this body where I spend my hot flashes. If I dared I would drift into the cooler, long hallway that separates our spaces and gaze at the action on the street below. I leave my door open to let the air flow but even my reading light reaching through my doorway bothers your light sleep. So I read from my tablet instead of my paperback and glimpse the outdoors with my ears.

So many rules to be followed. So many bright yellow pitchers to fill.

The first time I email my niece I tell her that I am infatuated, with Barcelona and with you. I recount the birthday celebration you made for me and the day spent at Park Güell, an expansive Gaudí masterpiece. You'd waited to see it so we could share the experience. I tell her how you led me through the streets of Barceloneta, that little residential neighbourhood of five- or six-storey buildings and narrow streets where locals are involved in the business of living: riding bikes, carrying groceries, stopping to speak with neighbours, children playing ball with their friends. I tell her I would like to return with her someday and stay in this district. But I notice there are banners that hang from windows telling tourists they are not welcome. Being so close to the beach they have been inundated with people like us, who rent short-term accommodations on Airbnb, infiltrating and threatening their community.

Writing to Gracie the next time, I refer to you as complicated, as inconsistent. And the next time I explain "complicated." Complicated is your vegan, organic diet coupled with your five cups of coffee and accompanying pastries each day. You preach healthy choices when I order my third martini and pontificate animal rights to my mouthful of foie gras. Yet you keep a rabbit foot for good luck. Complicated is your relationship with money, how you carry a notebook and pen to detail every penny you spend, how you panicked last night when you returned home with five Euros less than you could account for.

You sat down to fifteen minutes of meticulous calculations when we returned from your generous celebration of my birthday: dinner at Pitarra, a concert at the opera house, a purse you bought for me at Desigual and filled with chocolates, and a rose purchased at the table. When we got home you took out your notebook to record every penny you'd spent on me. Do you remember how much I paid for the violinist who serenaded you during dessert? you asked.

Complicated is your grief after the accidental death of your five-year-old daughter thirty years ago.

I awake late, a little hungover. You are at the kitchen sink, your breakfast of toast, almonds, and coffee on the table, untouched.

Thank you, I say. Yesterday was perfect, magic. I can't believe you did all that for me. I kiss your cheek.

Your body is as still and contained and dripping as an ice carving. It hunches over the sink, supported by your hands that dissolve into the enamel. Your silence, thick and abrupt, absorbs my words. All that moves is your melting face, shiny streams down your cheeks, drops from your nose drowning your mouth. Your tongue slinks out to lick your lips. I wipe my arm over my own lips, soaked with the tears I kissed off your cheek.

What? What is it? I think, If I touch her she will shatter. I step back out of the heat coming off your frozen body.

What did I do?

You take a few steps to the table and I see the photographs. Today is her birthday, you tell me, and you sob as though you have just discovered her body in the swimming pool.

But you didn't find her floating there yourself. She was not in my care, you tell me, as though pleading with me to judge you kindly.

She looks like you. She has, had, your green eyes. You must have put lipstick on her for this photo. Did you braid her hair yourself?

I try to understand but it has been three decades. Drink your coffee, I tell you.

I left her with my brother's wife, you are saying. I was in Rome. In Rome. I travelled. For work. Executive. Hilton. Important. She stayed with them. They had a child her age, a boy. She stayed with them.

I reach across and touch your cold coffee cup. I try to imagine the horror. The drugged, endless trip back from Italy. You don't tell me if you travelled alone. I imagine you alone, having to sit in the middle seat that long, endless way between two strangers. Men, businessmen, who look at you in your white business suit and white high heels that you don't kick off throughout the inert white flight. They think they are in a movie when you sit down between them like Princess Grace. They do not notice that your perfume is missing and your fingernail is split. So far from them, even an inch away, but each of them writes you into his script.

I really have to eat. How long have we been sitting here? You talking. Me imagining.

I can't imagine, I tell you. That long plane trip, I say.

Endless, you whisper.

Thirty years? I think.

You haven't moved when I come back from the bathroom, the photos of your daughter still disarranged in front of you, overlapping, fragments of eyes and noses and mouths, like dead leaves that need to be raked up and discarded. I want to reach down, separate them, spread them out and turn them around to see them clearly. I want to scoop them up and dump them in the compost bin to decompose.

I don't want to be here with you and your past. Will you notice if I just leave, go to the beach by myself? I want to walk out the door, but there is the problem of the key, the lock, my bruised arm.

When I sit down to rejoin you at the table your stories continue. You are home but you haven't seen her yet. You see her, frozen and dead. You have her body cremated. I think, Yes, it would take a lifetime to resolve this loss. I will let go of my swim. I will give you one day.

You dig a photo out of the pile. Your daughter grins with a missing tooth and bright pink lipstick outside the lines. You pull out a picture of a stuffed llama, a lizard, and a leopard. She went through the alphabet, you explain, each day taking a photo to make an alphabet chart on her wall. You find a photo of her with a fish, "F," and another one with jellybeans, "J."

So creative, I tell you.

Gifted, you respond, she was only four.

She only got to "J," you tell me, I finished it for her.

You search for the rest of the alphabet in the mass of photos in front of you and put them in order. All the ones before "K" are of your daughter surrounded by things she collected, except "C," where she is by herself, Christy.

She put on her princess gown for that one and got me to shoot it, you tell me between sobs.

The letters that come after, the photos you took, have just lonely objects. You are searching frantically for the "P" picture. P is for panic, I think. Panic. Pathetic. Perturbation. Pathos. You find it, a panda bear. It is stuck to the back of "O," little girl's overalls, an Easy-Bake oven. As the crisis subsides you gulp and pant, recovering air.

Someday I want to put these together in an album, one of those small ones, to make a little alphabet book, you say.

That would be nice, I respond.

Thirty years later? Honey, it's not going to happen, I think.

I get up and walk to the window, look down at the street life below. I am yearning for the water I can see at the edge of the cityscape.

Come to the beach; it will heal you, I say. You look at me as though I have punched you.

The fridge is empty.

The fridge is empty, I tell you, I'm going out to get groceries. I'll come back and make us some lunch.

You make your way over to your bed and lie down, facing the wall.

—

Outside, the streets are shimmering in the midday sun and vibrating with August tourists. I pass through corridors of Spanish and German and French. I am going to the beach first. Like a truant schoolgirl I tell myself that I am free to do what I want. I say, out loud, I don't care. I have no beach gear but I don't care and I leave my pile of clothes, backpack, money exposed on the burning sand.

When I come out of the water I stand like a statue to sun-dry, looming over the prone bodies. It's like one of those nightmares, suddenly naked in a crowd. I don't have your company to clothe me, and with no wind the sun is painfully slow to dry me even as it burns my skin. I did not swim well. Haunted by images of Christy I didn't feel the rocking of the water or the easing of my body. I am thirsty but I don't have the courage to signal to the water peddler passing by or to walk to the showers less than thirty metres away. I put my clothes on over my sticky carcass. I dread going back to you and your little girl.

You are not home and I still can't make my key work. When you finally arrive at dinnertime you find me asleep on the doorsill, your doormat. You could wipe your feet on me and I would not protest, I am so relieved to see you, to be let into our flat, to unload the groceries I brought home, which are as wilted as I. There is no sign of your breakfast or the photos that covered the table. As I empty the bags you stand over me picking up each item and putting it down again, whispering: lettuce, cheese, parsley, pomegranate, buns. You step closer and, like a feral animal, you sniff me, smell the sea on me, smell my secret swim. You don't say the word *betrayal*, but you pick up an apple, bite into it, put it down, and walk away.

These are the things I think, but do not to say to you, as we mumble past each other in the silent rooms.

Where were you? When did you go out?

Why did you leave me locked out for so long?

I swam. I left you alone and went to the beach. I had a good swim. A great swim.

Are you okay now?

Are you hungry? I'm hungry.

Is it like this every year or just on the decade anniversaries?

We have to do something about this key thing. We could get a locksmith, change the lock.

I shouldn't have left you alone with your grief.

Do you know what a passive-aggressive bitch you are?

I'm so sorry about your daughter. I had no idea.

You need to get a local cellphone plan so I can call you to let me back in.

I need to find another place.

I can't take this.

Why are you resisting getting a local plan?

You have no idea how this key thing is insane for me.

I'm not going to France with you next week. I'm done. I'm going home.

Your daughter, so beautiful. How did you bear it?

Do you know how controlling you are?

Thirty years, for fuck's sake. Get a life.

I'm leaving. I'm leaving. I'm leaving.

I'm so sorry.

Four more days. We sit at the table after breakfast and dinner, each with our iPads, sending and receiving emails from stable, supportive, faraway people. We don't share stories, talk and laugh about our day together, or share excitement in planning the next day. When we go out I follow you around, a cloud. Should we go to the gardens? you ask. Sure. Do you want to have tapas tonight? Okay. I still haven't told you. You still think I will be going with you when we leave this flat and rent the car. Three more days. I have to tell you. I waver, thinking I could handle the road trip with you, that I am giving up an opportunity. I think, I can do it. I stay home at night and go to bed before you get back from the Barcelona nights we used to share. I start packing. In the morning you go out and return with a large bag of groceries, taking money out of our grocery pool. You insist that I review the bill while you put the items away. Two packages of tofu, two litres of milk, a half-dozen apples, half a kilo of cheese, crème caramel, a litre of ice cream.

What is all this stuff? We're leaving the day after tomorrow.

There was nothing left. We still have to eat.

But you bought enough food here to last a week. We'll never be able to eat a quarter of this.

We can pack it for the road trip.

Ice cream? And I tell you I'm not going.

You sit down with a spoon and eat all the ice cream and drink the milk right out of the carton.

One more day. We are cleaning the apartment. Tomorrow the owner returns and we are supposed to pick up the car. My flight is at six in the morning. I know you are furious but you are not dramatic. Tears, only your damn tears, pouring out of your face. When I wake at four I walk past your bed lugging my suitcase. It sounds like a train wreck. Of course you are awake and you will get up to lock the door behind me. But for now you don't move.

ROWAN McCANDLESS

CASTAWAYS

M r. Papadakis tells us to smile. He says, "Girls, here at Castaways, we're not just selling Singapore Slings and Crab Rangoon. We're selling fantasy. We're giving a bunch of poor saps who've never been anywhere special a taste of tropical paradise right here on the Prairie. And you, young ladies, are key to the illusion. You're the dusky jewels in Castaways' crown . . . Yes, Tina. Even you. So you can stop rolling your eyes. Now, where was I?"

"Dusky jewels," I say, duct-taping my coconut bra into place.

"Oh yes, dusky jewels. Thank you, Amber."

"Uh huh. Whatever."

I fiddle with my bikini top. I gotta make sure "the girls" stay in place so there's no more unfortunate wardrobe malfunctions, like what happened last month in front of the Rotary Club.

"You're the dusky jewels in Castaways' crown," Mr. Papadakis says.

I test the duct tape by jumping up and down. Tina joins in. So does Janine, and my best friend, Enza. We bounce up and down, wiggle and jiggle like crazy, cuz being charged with public nudity ain't as much fun as you'd think.

Mr. Papadakis turns beet red. He mops his forehead. "You . . . you are . . . you're—"

"Delicate orchids," we say. "The exotic blooms in Castaways' floral lei."

Talk about your total bull-crap. I mean, there's nothing authentic or native about our South Seas Polynesian Revue. Like, Tina's native, but, you know, not that kinda native. Janine's fresh off the boat from some country that no longer exists. Enza's frickin' Italian. And me? I'm a Heinz 57. A little bit of everything and a whole lotta wasted potential, according to Mom.

Janine spritzes her hair with Sexi Hold Hairspray. Sexi Hold Hairspray promises to hold your hair like nobody's business. So does Enza, as she bulldozes over a chair and puts Janine in a headlock.

"Bitch," Enza says. "I told you to keep your hands off my shit."

"Whatchu talkin' 'bout, Willis?" Janine says.

Janine's still learning English. Picks a lot of it up watching television.

Tina's all WWF, pacing the linoleum, totally psyched to get tagged.

"Ow. Ow. Ow!" Janine says. "Please don't squeeze the Charmin!"

Janine drops the can.

I elbow Mr. Papadakis. Point at the clock.

He looks at the time, then claps his hands.

"Girls," he says. "Places."

Our grass skirts rustle on our race to the exit. Janine shoves right in front of me and I wind up last in line and the first girl Mr. Papadakis pinches on the ass tonight. FYI, we don't call him Papa Dick behind his back for nothing. So thanks, Janine. Thanks a frickin' lot.

At least the tips are good. Especially around this time of year. 'Tis the season. Ho. Ho. Ho. And it beats plucking chickens at the Castle Brand processing plant, which is where most people wind up in this piece-of-crap town. So when Papa Dick says, Now get out there, girls, and shake what your mamas gave you, we do.

We shake it across the wooden bridge surrounded by koi ponds, artificial tropical plants, and flaming bamboo torches. We shimmy beneath the night sky painted on the ceiling. Hula past the recirculating waterfall, the ginormous tiki statues belching smoke, and all the losers getting sloshed on Rum Rickies and Mai Tais.

We do the dance of the mysterious volcano god, the mysterious sea turtle, the mysterious coconut that just landed on our heads—and ya, you're right, we just make shit up as we go along.

Halfway through our performance, Papa Dick takes centre stage. "And now," he says, "Castaways' exotic beauties would love to share some of their island, ahem, magic with a few lucky patrons."

Customers laugh. There's wolf-whistling. Man, I frickin' hate audience participation time.

Me and the girls pass out cheap floral garlands made outta

plastic. Some balding, middle-aged jerk with bad breath grabs me around the waist and asks how much I charge for a lei—nudge nudge wink wink, like I haven't heard that line like a bazillion times before. I pry loose, thinking if I hadda dollar for every drunk d-bag that tried that line on me, I'd be so loaded I wouldn't have to work in this dump.

The girls start pulling people up from the audience. Janine zeroes in on some salesman, in town for the night, from Winnipeg. Tina and Enza duke it out over a stud-muffin celebrating a birthday. Me? I'm attached. My boyfriend's name is Kyle. So I drag up this elderly couple, try and convince them that doing the hula is actually pretty doable after hip replacement surgery.

I gotta say they're a sad and sorry sight. Not even three hours of drink specials during Happy Hour's enough to loosen them up. When my gran was alive, she'd say white folks wouldn't know rhythm if it came and slapped them right upside the head. Said they're all stiff and rigid cuz of that rod shoved up their ass. I loved Gran to bits, but she was like soooo prejudiced. Made me wonder, did she think the same about me, or at least about the half of me that's white?

When the show's over, we pose for photographs with customers. Split the profits 50-50 with Papa Dick, who acts as the photographer. You'd be surprised how many guys are willing to spend ten bucks just to have a photo taken with a couple of half-naked girls in hula outfits—or maybe not.

At the end of my shift, I punch out with $65 in tips and two phone numbers. The money I stuff in my purse. The phone numbers I give to Enza. They'll wind up written in Sharpie on a half-dozen bathroom stalls around town. Added to

Enza's "great wall of douchebaggery." *Call Nico. Fred. Ted.* Et cetera. *Loves to cheat on wife. Girlfriend. Taxes . . .* you get the picture.

"How many didja get tonight?" I say.

"Four d-bags for the wall," Enza says. "And one for me. The hottie from table seven."

"Bull-crap," says Tina.

"Bitch, I know you ain't calling me a liar," says Enza.

"Bitch, I know you ain't calling me a bitch," Tina replies.

"I'd like to teach the world to sing in perfect harmony," Janine says.

Tina glares. "Shut up, Janine."

So does Enza. "Ya, Janine. Zip it."

Janine tears up. Grabs a bag of Cheezie Puffs from outta her knapsack. "Don't hate me because I'm beautiful," she says.

I dab on some of Enza's patchouli oil and fetch my coat from the locker.

"Don't forget," I say to Enza. "The babysitter will have given Sammy-Jo supper. So it's just bath time and—"

"Snack, then a couple of books before bedtime," Enza says.

Tina nods, tells me not to worry.

"You're in good hands with Allstate," Janine says. She gives me a thumbs-up. Her fingertips are Day-Glo orange.

Enza sighs. "You and Kyle are so rheumatic."

"No kidding," Tina says. "You're like Romeo and Juliet. Cross-eyed lovers and shit."

My family can't stand Kyle. They think he's a total loser. And I'm a little too tan for Kyle's parents' taste—if you catch my drift. They also think I'm a slut. That I got pregnant just to trap him. Which I most definitely did not.

I grab my things, tiptoe down the hall.

Papa Dick steps out of his office. "Mele Kalikimaka," he says, and points at the plastic mistletoe tacked above his door.

"Merry Christmas," I say, making a run for it.

Castaways is located in a strip mall across the street from a Petro-Can and a Motel 6. I wade through snowdrifts in the parking lot. The sound of snowplows echo in the distance like the last gasps of dinosaurs. Kyle's waiting for me in his van. His van kicks ass. Has an air-brushed mural of Smaug wrapped around the sides.

The door's locked.

"Open up," I say. "It's frickin' freezing outside."

Smaug lets loose a cloud of smoke as the passenger door opens. The van reeks of pot. Kyle's eyes are bloodshot. Almost as red as Smaug's.

I climb in. Slam the door.

"You're blitzed," I say. "Again."

"No shit," Kyle says with a laugh.

I shake my head. "At this rate, we'll never save up enough money to get a place of our own."

"Aw, you know you love me."

He's right. I do. Regardless. In spite of. Which Mom says is proof positive that I don't have the brains God gave a gerbil.

We play tonsil hockey for a little while and then head over to his place. Well, actually his parents' place. They're gone for the weekend. Went to visit the KKKs—Kyle's sister, Kimberly, her husband, Kevin, and their six-month-old daughter, Kelly, over in the next town. No shit. That's what they call them-selves . . . the frickin' KKKs, which I think, at a minimum, is kinda insensitive. Kyle says I'm taking things the wrong way. That his family's not like that, that people aren't like that here in the Great White North. I think, Easy for him to say, cuz for people like me, unlike people like him, living in the Great White North ain't always so great.

We have a couple of beers in the kitchen. Make out a little, then head upstairs. There's this huge gallery wall next to the staircase. Kyle and his family on vacation. At Christmas. Celebrating birthdays and graduations. Man, I've never seen so many pictures of people wearing cardigans in all my life. There's not a hair out of place, not a single zit. They look like the model family photograph that comes in the frame when you buy it at the store. The one you pull out and replace with your own crappy snapshot from your own crappy life. There's, like, a ton of pictures of the KKKs. Guess how many photos there are of me and Sammy-Jo? Zero. Nada. Squat.

Kyle's room looks like a bomb went off.

I'm lying in bed, wearing my grass skirt from Castaways and nothing else.

Kyle's naked, except for the Polaroid camera draped around his neck. He's jumping on the mattress. His thing bobs up and down, like one of those dashboard ornaments. My tits are bouncing like crazy.

"Stop jumping," I say.

Kyle straddles me. He points the camera in my direction. His you-know-what's pointing too.

"Smile," he says.

I do. I don't mean it. I can't stop thinking about that frickin' gallery wall. How it's like some stupid shrine to Kimberly's baby.

There's a whirr. A click. A chemical smell. The camera flash hurts my eyes. Kyle's covered in spots. He dives into bed beside me. The comforter makes a whooshing sound as he lands. He watches the Polaroid develop. I watch his spots disappear.

"God, Amber," Kyle says. "You've got great tits."

I grab the photograph. The image is kinda grainy. I'm overexposed and the colour's off. Story of my frickin' life.

Kyle leans back. "Smile."

I make a face at him instead.

He takes a picture anyways.

"You're gonna get rid of them?" I say.

"Sure . . . at some point."

"Whadda you mean, 'at some point'?"

Kyle grabs the Polaroid. Takes one last look. "Babe, a guy's got needs. It's just a little something to remember you by when we're apart." He places the photographs in the drawer of his nightstand. He nestles against my side. Starts feeling me up.

"No glove. No love," I tell him.

"But—"

"But nothing."

Kyle bitches. Grabs a rubber.

Too bad. So sad. But after having a kid at sixteen, I'd like to think that I've learned my lesson. So now he's got to wear a raincoat or forget it.

"You're my Tahiti sweetie," he says.

I turn away. "I told you to stop calling me that."

"Tahiti sweetie."

He starts nibbling on my ear.

I can feel his hard-on pressed against my thigh.

"I swear to God, Kyle. Keep that frickin' thing away from me."

"Fuck's sake, Amber. What's your problem?"

"I'm not in the mood."

"Since when?"

"Since right now."

"You're always in the mood."

Not always. I'm not like a nympho or anything.

Kyle frowns. Lights a joint. "We finally get some alone time and this is how you want to spend it?"

Can't help it. His parents want nothing to do with me? Fine. See if I care. But Sammy-Jo's a different story. She's three, and still hasn't met them. Kyle says they need time to adjust. I gotta say they're sure taking their sweet time about it.

We stare at the ceiling, the walls, and each other for what feels like forever—and then go back to doing it.

Before I can get the key in the lock, Enza swings the door wide open. In the background there's wailing, like someone's killing a cat.

"I thought you'd be gone the whole weekend," Enza says.

"What's wrong?" I say. "Is Sammy-Jo okay?"

"Sammy-Jo's fine. It's you-know-who that's the problem."

"No way."

"Way," Enza says.

I take off my coat and boots. Sammy-Jo waddles up, dragging my old doll. Poor Darling Dolly-Walks-A-Lot has really taken a beating over the years. What's left of her blond hair is all chopped to shit. There's permanent marker all over her face.

I pick Sammy-Jo up. Give her a hug. She's the one thing me and Kyle got right.

"She's baaack," Sammy-Jo whispers in my ear.

"Ya, I'm not dealing with it," Enza says. "You deal with it."

"Good luck!" Tina shouts from the living-room. "You're gonna need it!"

Tina's vegging on the couch with Janine, who's halfway through a container of ice cream. They're both in PJs, watching *Sesame Street*.

"It's not easy being green," Janine says.

I follow the sound of wailing down the hallway. Sammy-Jo trails behind. I knock on the bathroom door, tell my sister I'm coming in.

Donna's cross-legged on the floor. She's bawling. Got mascara and blue kohl eye shadow running down her face. She looks a whole lot worse than poor Darling Dolly-Walks-A-Lot.

"I . . . hate . . . them," Donna says through tears. "I'm not . . . going back. You . . . can't . . . make me."

I nudge Sammy-Jo. "Auntie needs a hug."

Sammy-Jo looks at Donna, lets out a scream and takes off. There's this *kathunk kathunk kathunk* from Dolly's head banging on the floor.

"What're you . . . doing home?" Donna says.

"Change of plans."

"What happened?"

I tell Donna his parents came home early. I don't mention how Kyle frickin' kicked me out of bed and snuck me out the window. I hand Donna a tissue. She blows her nose, gives me some advice.

"Amber, you're not doing yourself any favours. You gotta dump that loser."

Like she should talk. Donna's got a thing for trouble. Me? I got a thing for Kyle. Her social worker says it's cuz we both suffer from low self-esteem, which Mom says is garbage. She figures the only thing we're suffering from is a severe case of stupid.

The phone rings.

Enza shouts my name.

Donna lights a smoke. "If that's Mom, you tell that bitch I'm not talking to her."

Ya, well you're not the only one—not that it matters. I head for the kitchen and the wall-mounted telephone, next to the refrigerator.

Enza holds out the receiver. Rolls her eyes.

There's this squawk on the line.

"Mom?"

More squawking.

My mom can't stand Enza. Thinks she's a bad influence, as if juvenile delinquency was catchy, like a case of influenza.

When me and Kyle met, a few years back, it was at a wedding social for one of Enza's cousins. I was sitting at a table with a fake ID and Enza. Kyle was there with friends. He was staring at me real hard. I thought he was cute. He thought I was Italian. "Take a picture," I said. "It'll last longer." Kyle pretended to do just that. The rest, as they say, is history—or my downward slide into damnation, depending on who you ask.

"Mom . . . Mom!" I wrap the phone cord around my neck, pretend to strangle myself.

"Amber? Is that you?"

I untangle the cord.

"Yup."

"You tell that Enza she's going straight to Hell."

I shake my head. Mom's been this way ever since she found religion through Reverend Ray.

"Mom."

"What?"

"Donna's bawling her eyes out in my bathroom. What's going on?"

I hear my stepdad preaching in the background.

Dad took off when we were little and we haven't seen him since. Mom was at a loss, raising two kids on her own. Until the Reverend Ray showed up and married her, and took us under his wing. Mom calls him her "personal Ray of sunshine." He calls her naive for having married outside her race, calls us ungrateful brats, a couple of coloured Whores of Babylon.

"Mom, tell Ray to shut the fuck up."

"Language," she says. "You know the Reverend doesn't mean anything by it. He only has your best interests at heart."

"Sure . . . whatever you say."

"The Reverend says he's praying for both you girls."

"Mom?"

"What?"

"When you coming by to pick up Donna . . . Hello? Hello?"

Waikiki Wednesdays suck. Seriously, they blow. But renting a cute little bungalow won't come cheap, so it doesn't matter if Waikiki Wednesdays suck, which they totally do, or that I'm under the weather with a severe case of stupid, which may or may not be accurate. "The show," as they say, "must go on."

At least that's what Papa Dick said right after firing Janine. The show must go on, which is how I got the extra hours. Poor Janine. She was getting kinda chunky around the middle. And Papa Dick says we cater to a certain clientele. Respectable businessmen who work hard for their money and don't want to be staring at jelly bellies while they're eating their poi poi platters and drinking Hawaiian Sunsets. If jelly bellies is what they wanted they'd go home to their wives after work.

I feel like a traitor but Janine understands. Mom and Ray gave Donna the boot. So now, on top of everything, my fifteen-year-old sister's my responsibility.

The hostess stand is too close to the door. I got goosebumps in places I oughta not have them. I think my lips are turning blue. Have they turned blue? I pucker up. Change my mind, cuz the guys from Castle Brand's head office are piling in, and I don't want to give the wrong impression.

I'm freezing. Seriously, like in or out. But close the frickin' door already. I wish I had a parka, or a sweater. Man, I'd even settle for a scarf and a pair of garbage gloves. But rules are rules. Gotta follow the script.

"Welcome to Castaways. We'd love to get you lei'd."

There are two malls in town. The good mall and the bad mall. The good mall's shiny and clean. Harte's Portrait Studio's located in the good mall. The good mall's in the better part of town, unlike the bad mall, which's in the worst. Guess where you'll find Castaways? If you picked the good mall, you might wanna guess again.

Kyle was supposed to drive us, but something came up.

So, he's going to meet us at Harte's. The good mall's packed. Christmas carols play over the loudspeakers. Everyone's in a shopping frenzy.

"You better stick to me like glue," I tell Donna.

"But I wanna look at stuff," she says.

"Like glue."

"What good's coming to the mall if I can't even buy stuff?"

"You got any money?"

"No."

"Then end of discussion."

I gotta get Sammy-Jo outta her snowsuit without her taking a hissy-fit. Donna wanders off. So does Sammy-Jo.

"Get back here," I say, and they both start whining.

I unzip zippers, unbuckle buckles, stuff Sammy-Jo's toque and scarf into the sleeves of her snowsuit. She's got hat head. And what the frick happened to her green barrettes? The ones matching her velvet dress that cost me a week in tips.

In the middle of the mall is Santa's Village. There's an oversized rocking chair in front of a fake log cabin covered in polyester rolls of artificial snow and mini-lights.

"I wanna see Santa," Sammy-Jo says.

There's a winding lineup of parents and kids, being herded like cattle.

"Later," I tell her.

By the time we get to the portrait studio, Sammy-Jo's in tears cuz she hasn't seen Santa, Donna's pockets are crammed with five-finger discounts, I've got a frickin' headache and Kyle's nowhere in sight.

Harte's is real professional-looking. Lots of pictures of happy families.

Sammy-Jo drops to the floor, starts kicking and screaming for Santa and a candy cane and a unicorn and whatever else pops into her head.

"Every moment is precious," some guy named Franklin says from behind the counter. "Shouldn't your portraits be too?"

I'm wearing a little black dress. I think I look hot. And I told Kyle, to make up for sneaking me outta the window, he'd better show up in a suit and tie. Which reminds me. Where the frick is he? I say we have an appointment. Tell Sammy-Jo, enough already. Search my purse for the Harte's Holidaze Coupon I cut outta the flyer.

Franklin hauls out a binder. "You have a choice of photographic backgrounds."

Mom tried for years to get a decent family portrait of us. But it never worked out. One year me and Donna got chicken pox. The next year it was the mumps. Year after that, Mom shipped us back to Truro to live with Gran. And so it went. It wasn't intentional or anything. Just like me getting knocked up at fifteen. No way was I having my picture taken. I wound up looking like a frickin' beached whale. Besides, Mom and Ray kicked me out once they found out I was pregnant, so getting a family portrait was kinda moot.

I find my coupon, but can't decide on the backdrop. I ask Donna what she thinks, but she couldn't care less. Sammy-Jo's busy with her tantrum. And Kyle's still not here to offer an opinion.

I nix the tropical beach. Decide on a winter scene with a sled.

"Good choice," Franklin says, and leaves to set things up.

Donna bribes Sammy-Jo off the floor with lip gloss.

"Don't put that crap on her face."

"Take a chill pill," Donna says. "Pucker up, Buttercup."

She pretends to add lip gloss. Sammy-Jo smacks her lips.

"Everything's ready," Franklin says. "If you'll please come this way."

"We can't. My boyfriend's not here yet."

"Kyle's not here," Donna says. "Surprise. Surprise."

"Kyle's a dick," Sammy-Jo says.

Donna laughs.

My kid starts running in circles. "Kyle's a dick. Kyle's a dick."

Donna's in tears, she's laughing so hard.

"Stop encouraging her. Sammy-Jo, don't talk like that about your father."

"Maybe he should act like one," Donna says.

"Maybe *you* shouldn't be teaching Sammy-Jo to call her father a dick."

Franklin clears his throat. "Every moment is precious. But I really don't have time for this."

"He'll be here any minute," I say.

"Really," Franklin says. "I'd like to accommodate you but—"

"Any minute." And I flop into a chair.

Donna reads to Sammy-Jo. I watch the clock, flip through magazines.

I catch up on celebrity gossip. Pick up tips on how to get the most kissable lips. Although, it's not like Kyle's gonna benefit cuz by now I'm totally pissed. I check out flyers. Give Sammy-Jo a juice box.

Donna yawns. "Ten bucks Kyle's a no show."

"He'll be here," I say.

I give Donna an evil look. And a half-hour later, ten one-dollar bills.

On Friday, two women from the Ladies' Auxiliary of the Immaculate Deception show up at our door. One's sprouted green felt antlers with bells and a flashing red nose. The other's wearing Spock ears and is dressed like Mrs. Claus. Both are carrying baskets filled to the brim with Christian charity.

"Merry Christmas," says Mrs. Claus.

"Joyeux Noël," says Rudolph.

"Who's there?" Tina shouts from the kitchen.

"It's freaks bearing gifts!"

Mrs. Claus gives me this look. Uh oh. I think I just got put on the naughty list.

Rudolph frowns, whispers to Mrs. Claus, "I thought this would be a lot more fun."

Tina rushes to the door. She looks forward to their visit every year. Gives her a chance to talk about religion, now that the Jehovah's Witnesses stay clear of our place.

"Come in," Tina says. "Please excuse the mess."

Mess. What mess? We've been scrubbing the place for days, used so much liquid disinfectant that the house reeks of pine, and we don't even have a tree up yet.

I step aside to let them in.

The Ladies' Auxiliary of the Immaculate Deception show up every year around this time. They come bringing frozen turkeys, boxes of instant mashed potatoes, expired pudding pie mix, and the promise of salvation. Every year, it's like the Island of Misfit Toys under the Christmas tree.

"There's more out in the car," Rudolph says.

I grab my coat, slip on boots. I hate having to rely on the kindness of strangers. I wish Kyle would step up, frickin' show up for a change. I don't want Sammy-Jo growing up with slunkys instead of slinkys under the Christmas tree, pamphlets about fire and brimstone stuffed in her stocking.

The driveway's slippery. I wipe out beside their car.

"You okay?"

"I'll survive."

The voice belongs to a sexy elf with bleached-blond hair. She's holding a turkey. There's something vaguely familiar. Not about the turkey but the elf. Oh shit. It's you-know-frickin'-who. I stand and brush myself off. I grab a box from the trunk, hoping she doesn't recognize me.

"You sure you're all right?"

"Positive."

We head toward the house.

"Don't we know one another?" she says.

"I don't think so."

We drop off the turkey and a box of hand-me-downs. Enza and Janine are singing carols with Mrs. Claus. Tina's debating with Rudolph the likelihood of some virgin giving birth in a manger. We head back to the car.

"I've got it. You went to JHC. I never forget a face. Or a name. It's Amethyst, right?"

"Wrong."

"Quartz?"

Quartz? Bitch, seriously?

"It's Amber."

"Amber . . . That's it. I knew it was something different. It's me. Karen Russell. Don't you remember? We had a couple of grade ten classes together. I mean, we did, until you disap-peared second semester. Weren't you going out with Kyle Reimer back then?"

"I was. I still am."

"Huh . . . You don't say."

I do say. Like fuck off, bitch.

"Say what?" Donna asks.

Donna's holding a saw in one hand, the trunk of a Christmas tree in the other. She's covered in pine needles. So's the sidewalk.

"Karen made fun of me in high school."

Karen shakes her head. Bells jingle. "I don't think so."

"Ya, you did. You used to call me halfro, watermelon bum."

"Is she the one?" Donna asks.

I nod.

"You're mistaken," Karen says.

"Whoreo Cookie," me and Donna say together.

"Look . . . I'm just in town for the holidays. I'm only trying to help my mother spread a little Christmas cheer."

"Is that what they're calling the clap nowadays?" Donna says.

I laugh.

Karen glares, starts using words no respectable elf would say.

"Where's the beef?" Janine shouts from the stoop.

Karen stomps toward the front door.

"Where'd the tree come from?" I say to Donna.

"Do you really want to know?" she says.

My mom's such a know-it-all. Tells me Kyle's never gonna buy the cow when he can get the milk for free. So not only am I a slut, but I'm a stupid slut. Which is why Donna's the master-mind, Janine's the driver, Enza and Tina are on lookout, and

I'm on the fence. We're parked a few houses down from Kyle's place. It's late at night. The lights are off at the house and there's no vehicles in the driveway.

"I dunno. I still think this is a bad idea."

Donna shakes her head.

"Oh my God," she says. "Will you grow a pair already?"

"What if we get caught?"

"We're not going to get caught."

"We're on a mission," Janine says. "A mission from God."

Enza nods. "Ain't that the mother-fucking truth."

Tina high-fives Janine, and she smiles. It's good to see Janine smile again. She's been kinda depressed lately, thanks to her new job executing chickens for Castle Brand, and the vegetarian diet she's gone on to get her job back at Castaways.

"He's gonna know it was me," I say. "What if he goes to the cops?"

"Go to the cops?" Enza says. "And what's he gonna tell 'em?"

"No kidding," Tina says. "Excuse me, officer, but my ex stole the stash of nudie pics I took of her."

Donna's getting restless in the front seat. "We doing this or what?"

"Maybe he got rid of them like he promised."

"Sure," Donna says. "Cuz, if there's one thing we know about Kyle, is he's the kinda guy who keeps his word."

"Nobody puts baby in the corner," Janine says.

Kyle was supposed to go with me to my staff Christmas party. Instead, he cancelled and went on a ski trip with his family. Said he needed a break cuz I'm too demanding. I told him to fuck off. That the only thing I needed from him were the Polaroids back.

"Keep the engine running," I say.

Me and Donna get out of the car. I'm wearing a low-cut, sparkly cocktail dress under my coat. I can't stop shivering. It's cold. Plus, I'm frickin' nervous about this whole B and E situation.

Donna weaves her way toward the house. I try and keep up but I'm kinda at a disadvantage. I'm wearing four-inch heels and I downed way more B-52s than she did.

Donna falls into a snowbank.

I stumble over.

"Holy crap. Are you okay?"

My sister laughs. "Help, I've fallen and I can't get up."

She starts making a snow angel.

I yank her to her feet.

"What about footprints?" I say, pointing at the trail behind us.

"I've got an idea," Donna says, and we walk single file, backwards, into the yard.

The spare key's right where it always is, in the gazebo above the doorjamb. I got butterflies in my stomach. I unlock the door. Feel like I'm gonna barf a little. We step inside. Donna turns on a flashlight. I turn off the alarm.

"Lead the way," Donna says, shining the flashlight. We head down the hall. Halfway up the winding staircase, she comes to a halt.

"Man," Donna says. "Now, that's what I call a crime scene."

"Motherfucker," I say. There's a ginormous new portrait hanging on the wall. Kyle and his family wearing identical holiday sweaters.

"It looks like Christmas fucking threw up all over them," Donna says.

We get to the top of the stairs.

"Which way?"

"Follow me."

We head for Kyle's bedroom. Step inside.

Donna sits on the edge of the bed. "So this is where the magic happens," she says, dropping a pair of Kyle's boxers onto the floor.

"Ha," I say. "Very funny."

I head for the nightstand. Open the drawer. Inside, there's a pile of mismatched socks, a stash of rubbers, and some rolling papers.

"They're not here," I say. "What am I doing? This is stupid. What if he got rid of them like he promised?"

"This is Kyle we're talking about. Remember?"

She gets up, starts rifling through his dresser.

I trade places and lie down.

"Anything?"

"Nope," Donna says.

I get bed spins. Turn on my side.

Donna searches Kyle's closet, tossing clothes onto the floor. It reminds me of when we were little. Mom started drinking after Dad left. Like, a lot. After she'd pass out, me and Donna would comb the house for hidden bottles. Dump the contents of whatever we found down the sink. Mom was good at hiding her booze, but my sister was better at finding it.

"Up," Donna says.

I get off the bed. Lean against the wall cuz I'm feeling a little woozy. Donna gropes along the mattress edge, looks under the bed. Finds nothing but dust bunnies and clothes way overdue for laundry.

"Give me a hand."

I help lift the mattress.

"Hurry up," I say. "This thing weighs a ton."

"Jackpot," Donna says. She grabs an envelope from between the mattress and box-spring. I drop the mattress and take the envelope from Donna.

"Motherfucker," I say. "Kyle frickin' swore he got rid of them."

The envelope's worn around the edges and wrapped with an elastic. I remove the rubber band. Donna shines the flashlight and I peek inside.

"I'm gonna be sick," I say.

I run to the can. Puke in the toilet.

"You okay?" Donna says, as I rinse my mouth with water from the tap.

"No. Not really." I give her the envelope. Seems I'm not the only one Kyle's been playing dress-up with.

Donna starts flipping through snapshots.

"What a Grade A douche-bag," Donna says. "Isn't that . . . ?"

"Yup." Looks like Karen Russell still fits her cheerleading outfit from JHC.

"I wanna go home."

"Not yet," Donna says, and drags me back to Kyle's bedroom.

I watch her poke holes in Kyle's condoms. Pocket his hash pipe and rolling papers. She starts trashing the bedroom.

"Come on," Donna says. "It'll make you feel better."

I do. But it doesn't.

Kyle's camera's on the floor, next to the bed. Donna picks it up.

"Say cheese," she says. I do. I also double-flip the bird.

There's a whir. A click. A chemical smell.

Once the photo's developed, I tuck it under Kyle's mattress.

"Merry Christmas," I say, making a run for it.

I'm almost outta tears and the gas tank's close to empty. So we stop at a filling station on the way home.

Janine gets out to pump gas.

It's snowing. Looks pretty against the streetlights. It's like we're trapped inside a snow globe that's been turned upside down and shaken.

"I'm gonna be sick."

I stumble outta the back seat. Stagger toward the can.

"Wait up," Tina says.

Enza and Donna chase after me. Tina's close behind.

Inside the filling station, it smells like rubber tires and old hot dogs.

"Merry Christmas, Enza," the clerk says from behind the counter.

"Merry Christmas, Jimmy," Enza says.

The can's disgusting. But beggars can't be choosers. Enza holds my hair while I woof my cookies into the toilet.

"She okay?" Donna asks.

"She will be," Tina says.

When I'm done, Enza flushes the toilet and helps me clean up in front of the sink.

The mirror's got this crack down the middle. Throws off my reflection.

"I'm soooo frickin' stupid."

"Fuck him," Enza says.

"Ya, to Hell with him," Tina says, leaning against sink. "It's his loss. Not yours."

Enza pulls out a Sharpie. She writes the letter K on the bathroom wall as Donna pulls a pack of Export As from outta her purse.

Donna lights a smoke. Takes a drag.

Enza adds the rest of Kyle's name to the graffiti-covered wall.

"Can I borrow your Bic?" I say.

My sister passes me her lighter. I grab the Polaroids from my coat pocket. Toss them into the sink as Janine walks into the can.

"This message will self-destruct in thirty-seven seconds," Janine says.

I set the Polaroids on fire. And under harsh fluorescent lights, we huddle together and watch them burn.

SHASHI BHAT

MUTE

Everyone was drunk. It felt like a Cheever story—or maybe I only thought that because he was all over the syllabus of our Character Development class, where the professor read stories aloud to us with beautiful enunciation and told us about the old days when he used to drink with Cheever. I felt as though I had ascended into this world where writers were real people you knew. I felt ashamed of having not yet published anything.

A month and a half earlier I'd moved to Baltimore to attend a graduate writing program. My classmates seemed overwhelmingly American; up until then I had lived in Halifax. Baltimore was a port city, but not like Halifax, where you always remembered you were near the ocean. In Baltimore you always remembered you were near drug crime. My classmates—there were nine of them—had New York or Southern accents, and they boomed over my head. Had I been this quiet in Canada? I couldn't remember. In bars, my classmates always knew what drinks to order and were decisive about where to sit or stand.

We were at a department reception at the faculty club. Rooms opened into rooms. Each room had a name: "The Nobel Room," "The Milton Eisenhower Room," etc. They had crown moulding on high ceilings and tall windows with pleated brocade curtains. All of the employees were African-American and dressed like Forest Whitaker in *Lee Daniels' The Butler*. They carried silver trays covered with bits of puff pastry and skewered scallops topped with pea sprouts and ginger miso cream. There was an open bar.

When I entered, I found five of my classmates discussing their midterm teaching evaluations. "I read mine after like half a bottle of limoncello," said Natasha, whose lipstick had left a perfect red half-lip on her wine glass.

"Mine were excellent overall," said Murphy, who was wearing a bowtie and speaking in a maybe-ironic voice. "I plan to address the constructive criticism over the next few weeks."

Most of them had received comments calling them inspiring and complimenting their clothing or facial features. I could only remember the two bad ones I'd received, one of which said, "Though the course has the word 'creative' in its title, the instructor does not seem like a creative person," and the other, "Spoke a lot, but said little."

A writer approached us. I had developed a vague crush on him and wished I wasn't clutching a crumpled napkin full of empty skewers. The writer was an alum who kept attending all of the department parties after graduating. The two older female secretaries fawned over him. In profile, his hair was a tilde—a perfect sideways wave. His novel concerned a fictional protagonist who was also a writer and the same age as him and single and had a sibling with Down syndrome. Before sleep I fantasized about lying to him and pretending that I, too, had a sibling with Down syndrome in order to woo him by way of our commonalities. This was what someone on a Netflix show would do. I, of course, would not do this—partly because it would be deceitful and unforgivable and strange in real life, but mostly because I would be too nervous about being caught in a lie.

Along with the writer came Professor Coates—an older, imposing man who was known to scream at people in his office when the door was closed. "A delight to see all of you," he said, raising his glass. He began with small talk—"How are you all settling in?"—and then segued into a discussion of the program's long history and espousing on its notable alumni. I sort of lost track, as I was looking at the black cocktail dresses of the other girls in the program and realizing that I was dressed quite wrong. Earlier, when I had come out of a bathroom stall, one of the secretaries had said to me, "Oh, Nina, I knew it was you from the shoes."

Professor Coates and the writer were discussing a short story, but I couldn't tell which one. My classmates were all throwing in excellent comments about the story's restraint of language and the unmatchable elegance of its ending; the writer made a pun involving the story's title that caused Professor Coates to laugh so hard he needed to hold his whiskey with both hands. By now, most of the class had gathered around, along with three faculty members. The air was filled with rhetoric.

"You—" said Professor Coates. I realized he was pointing at me. This was the first time he had spoken to me at all. Everyone turned in my direction, smiles depleting at his sudden shift in tone. "Why don't you contribute something to the conversation?"

I waited. I said nothing. I'd gone mute.

My apartment was infested. Every day I encountered a new insect, each leggier or craftier than the last. One morning I found a long house centipede curled in the water glass on my night stand. I had read that in Baltimore there were more rats than people. Online you could find an interactive map of health violations at local restaurants, and my neighbourhood was dotted with tiny rodent icons. In one section of the city, a garbage truck had sunken into the street, swarmed by rats that had eaten through the ground below.

There was a rumour that if you raised your arms above your head at night on campus, sensors would alert campus police. I lived past the reach of their protection. Each night a man across the street from me stood on his porch and yelled, "Where you going?" at anyone who passed. Once, when I'd ducked my head without answering, he'd followed me a few metres down the road. My right hand clutched my apartment key inside my pocket, ready to use as a weapon, and when I reached my building I walked past the door and around the block, back in the direction of campus, until I was sure he was gone. Now I used my building's basement door to avoid him. The basement held a leaking washing machine and a trembling dryer, and the cockroaches travelled in packs, like moving rugs. The abandoned bicycles of past tenants were piled into a sculpture against a wall.

When I first moved in I read the crime reports and thought about getting a gun. To calm myself I read Halifax newspapers.

The familiar pictures of columnists made my heart ache. I unpacked a box of undergraduate memorabilia and found a rape whistle with my old university's logo on it. I blew into it gently, and the sound was bird-like, unusually clear. The windows of my apartment didn't lock, so I used thick rope to tie them to my radiator. I'd started having sleep paralysis visions of people climbing into my window at night.

This was Baltimore.

On the Friday after the reception, I got a call from a guy in my program, Eli, who said a bunch of people were going to a bar called The Charles. He said that I should come along and that since we lived in the same area we should share a cab.

"Unless you already have plans?" he asked.

I'd been in the process of spreading Borax on the floor because I'd read that it was abrasive to a cockroach's exoskeleton. "Just a night in reading Faulkner."

"I'll call you when we leave here," he said.

I put heels on first, to stay high above the roaches. I had purchased the shoes after the department party and now lurched around my closet seeking a dress. A YouTube search yielded a makeup tutorial.

Once I was ready I went back to watching the MTV documentary show *Catfish*, where handsome young hosts Nev and Max helped teens investigate their online lovers. The lovers were often discovered to be an unexpected gender, race, weight, or height, or they had children or a glass eye. I empathized with everybody. As a teen in the late 1990s—before texting, instant messaging, Facebook, or Tinder—I'd formed these beautiful, epistolary email relationships with Australian men. I'd had one feverish and weird chatroom affair with a man in his forties. He phoned once, but I was too scared to speak and hung up the phone. I never logged in to that chatroom again.

Watching *Catfish*, I would weep into my keyboard as a kid explained how he'd been honest about everything except that one thing: his identity. "It was still me," he pleaded. The episode ended with an update in white text over the final image: "Chelsea and Marquise no longer speak. Chelsea has decided to look for a relationship outside the internet."

I watched two episodes of the show, but Eli didn't call. It was nearing 10:30, but how late did people go out in Baltimore? Probably later than in Halifax, I figured, remembering how I'd stumbled home at night over cobblestones, an arm thrown over a friend's shoulder, my hair frizzing in the inevitable fog. I watched another two episodes of *Catfish*. Then it was 11:30. I paced the carpet, and my heels left a blotchy trail of Borax. I thought about texting Eli but didn't. Maybe he did this on purpose, I thought, or, more likely—and more embarrassingly—he just forgot.

At midnight I washed off my makeup and went to sleep. In the morning, my phone had one notification: a Facebook message. Anxiety bloomed and swirled in my chest, but it was only my grandmother, who had become a social media expert since moving into a home a couple months earlier.

Mother's Day was lovely with all the loving notes, the little ones and my boys taking me out, and the orchid and carnations. Your dad even phoned from Fredericton. In short, it really was a nice day except that one of the

women I have become friendly with here died suddenly. Hope your day was good, too.

I felt like I'd been sucked into this Nabokov story we had to
teach in our intro classes, where all that happens is that this
kid has a really shitty day. He goes to a party at another kid's
family's estate and joins in a game of hide-and-seek, but while
he is hiding between a wardrobe and a Dutch stove the others
forget about him and abandon the game to picnic on bilberry
tarts. At the end of the story he imagines faking his own suicide to make everybody else feel bad. I read one of the lines
aloud in class—"One could hear a clock hoarsely ticktocking
and that sound reminded one of various dull and sad things"—
and then started laughing insanely. The students laughed
along with me in this magical millisecond of connection. I felt
so grateful that they got the joke.

That Saturday I escaped Baltimore. The Smithsonian had a
Jim Henson exhibit, so I took the Amtrak to Washington and
joined a tour group that stood in a semi-circle facing Kermit
the Frog in a glass box. His green felt body looked inanimate
and small next to all the humans, and the woman giving the
tour referred to Kermit as Henson's alter ego. While she
spoke, a scene from *Catfish* kept flashing in my head: this
lovely, honest, ginger-haired girl fell in online love with a guy
named Skylar, who turned out to be a guy named Brian, who
only wanted to "freshen up his game." Hosts Nev and Max
jointly eviscerated him.

"You understand this makes you look like a huge asshole,
right?" asked Nev, as he walked the girl away.

"Yeah, yeah," replied Brian.

"So you're literally fishing and hooking girls, then just kind of tossing them back into the ocean with scars?" asked Max, who stayed behind with the camera.

"It is what it is," said Brian.

Then Nev said to the girl, "You've got an opportunity now." He put an arm around her shoulder as they walked back to Brian. She spoke without stutter. She pointed out every crack in his sociopathic logic. She demanded to know why he did it. Her voice swelled like a crescendoing orchestra.

The tour group rounded a corner into a hall of more Muppets in glass cases. The guide said that to her this felt like coming home: "They taught us how to count, how to read . . ."

I heard somebody behind me ask, "So who's your favourite Muppet?"

When I turned, I saw this big guy grinning at me. My first thought was that he was so massive he could puppeteer Mr. Snuffleupagus. I wondered how long he'd been standing there, asking women this question. "Sweet-ums," I said.

"Which one is that?"

"He's the giant ogre," I told him. "In his first appearance he tried to eat Kermit, but later he mostly just sang Wagnerian operas." I had learned this minutes ago from a placard on the wall.

"Mine is Sam the Eagle," he said, "for his integrity." The guy had a dense black beard with fine wiry hairs; I thought of the Maritimes and the whittled wooden fishermen they sold at Peggy's Cove.

After the tour, as we wandered through the gift shop, I kept repeating in my head "Charles Etienne de St. Valery

Bon"—a name that I had memorized for a bizarrely specific weekly quiz. The inner chanting was calming. The big guy, whose name turned out to be James, read aloud from a children's book about an anthropomorphized stegosaurus, while I peered at turquoise and agate jewellery. We flipped through all the art posters in the rack, their plastic frames clacking together one by one.

"I hate to tell you this, but I have to get back to work," he said, motioning toward the door with his head because he had a souvenir magnet in each of his hands.

"Oh," I said. "It's Saturday." I imagined the next hour: taking the train home, turning the lights on in my apartment, watching the cockroaches scatter.

"I would love to make you a baked ziti sometime."

"Okay, sure," I said in an atonal stutter, but inside I was swooning—*baked ziti*. "I'm a vegetarian, though, and I live in Baltimore."

"No problem. Do you have an eight-inch square baking dish?" he asked.

He walked me to Union Station and said goodbye in a Kermit the Frog voice. On the train ride home I started mentally preparing a tiramisu. Out the window I saw a rat, but for once it was running in the opposite direction.

In the week before James made it to Baltimore, we had three euphoric phone conversations—conversations with no allusions to Philip Roth or drunken confessions or our fears of never getting published. He didn't even want to get published—he wanted a PhD in biochemistry. During our first phone conversation he told me that bee venom is acidic. I told him I'd never been stung by a bee, but as a child I was obsessed with the movie *My Girl*, in which Macaulay Culkin's character is stung, has an anaphylactic reaction, and dies. I'd watched the funeral scene repeatedly, rewinding my VHS copy in my parents' VCR.

That week I added a long scene to a story I was writing, in which a girl gets dumped by her boyfriend and then buys ice cream at a convenience store near Point Pleasant Park. As she sits on a bench by the ocean, she becomes so engrossed in the rare sight of a crested caracara that she lets the ice cream melt.

We workshopped it promptly that Friday—the same day James was scheduled to come to my place and bake ziti. The professor was a woman who spoke firmly and eloquently, as though her words had an underlying rhythm. She had brown hair cropped an inch below her ears and a clear gaze that looked through you along with whatever you'd written. On the back of your manuscript she'd write a one-sentence critique. Reading it, your mind would oscillate and fragment and flower into a billion ideas. Sometimes, when she spoke in class, she was so brilliant that it made my heart ache.

Next to her was a lanky guy named Tom, who said, "There's a real opportunity here in the symbolism, but I don't buy that she'd be distracted by a bird for so long that the ice cream would actually melt."

"I didn't know anything could melt in the Canadian climate," said Murphy, a charming, affable fellow whose last story had been about keeping a woman as a slave.

"Is it meant as hyperbole, do you think?" asked Natasha, the only other female in the class. She wore her scarf looped in ways I tried and failed to replicate.

"The whole thing is very lyrical, as your work always is," said Graeme, quiet and serious, nodding at me, "but the sentences are long. Aren't we past long sentences? But beautiful stuff, undoubtedly."

"Can a type of sentence go out of style?" asked the undergraduate at the end of the table, who was auditing the class and evidently hadn't read the story. Nobody had bothered to learn his name. He'd been drawing continuously through the discussion, and he'd sketched the professor in black felt-tip pen on his copy of the manuscript. It didn't do her justice.

All of our classes were held in a room at the top of a brick tower. It had five tall, hexagonal windows without screens. A bright orange oriole had once flown in, whistling and rustling around the top of the table before the caretakers managed to shoo him out again. Now the table had ten copies of my manuscript on it, dog-eared and scribbled over in various colours of ink. After the discussion they would hand their copies to me, and I'd go to one of those desks in the stacks of the library and read them one by one.

"I don't want to be prescriptive," said Tom, his long legs endlessly jiggling under the table, "but you gotta change the names of the twin brothers. One of their names, at least. Who gives twins rhyming names? Why would you do that?"

I could think of two pairs of twins with rhyming names: 1) on the TV show *The Bachelor*, where in season 15 bachelor Brad Womack had brought on his twin brother Chad to see if the women could tell the difference (they could), and 2) in a comic strip called "Ram and Shyam," a sort of Goofus and Gallant for the Indian Subcontinent. But I didn't say this. You weren't allowed to speak during your own workshop, though you had a chance at the end if you wanted to respond. The undergraduate used this as an opportunity to explain why everyone's criticisms of his story were incorrect. You could see him through the workshop not fully listening but storing up his responses like acorns in his cheeks.

Out one of the hexagonal windows I could see the grass of the quad and, farther beyond, an apartment building where F. Scott Fitzgerald had lived while Zelda convalesced in a nearby sanatorium. Our Character Development professor had told us this, gesturing to the building with his copy of *This Side of Paradise*, as I imagined Zelda writhing in a straitjacket worn over a flapper dress.

"The guy's motivations for breaking up with her don't make much sense," said Natasha. "He ends it because she refuses to ask for directions? Is this a gender thing?"

She was referring to a flashback scene in the story, where the couple travels to France and the girl wants to visit the best macaron shop in Paris, so they wander the 6th arrondissement but can't find it. The guy tells the girl that this is the perfect opportunity to practice her French by asking a passerby for directions, but she refuses and won't tell him why.

"Why won't she?" asked Murphy, and they all turned to me, even the professor.

I had the answer figured out when I was writing the story—mostly because the story was autobiographical. It had to do with fear, but also with having made fear into a habit for so long that it was now instinctual. I was trying to think of how to articulate this, but I felt as though I had a cold metal ball rolling in my throat. The professor looked me in the eye for a second before turning back to the page and writing something down.

After class I walked straight to one of the lower levels of the library (its floors went deep underground, so it was exceptionally quiet). I tucked myself into a study cubicle and read the scribbled comments on each copy of my story, sucking in my breath, saving the professor's for last. When I got to hers, I went through every page, noting each word she'd circled and each question mark in the margins. Then I flipped to the back to read her final remarks.

"You can do better," she'd written. And under that: "The best macaron shop in Paris is in the 12th arrondissement."

James brought a backpack full of vegetables and dry noodles. He had a baseball cap on, and it seemed like he'd changed his beard, trimming it significantly or maybe shaving part of it off. He and the backpack overwhelmed my kitchen alcove, which had enough room for a table the size of a bicycle wheel. Onto the table went the ingredients: a lump of mozzarella, a crisp white onion, a container of ricotta, and a paper bag full of mushrooms. I got out two cutting boards and two knives, and we began chopping—he on the table and me on the wedge of counter space. We hadn't really spoken yet, except hellos and a twenty-second apartment tour ("You own a lot of books!" he said). Prior to his arrival I'd swept up the Borax and put on every lamp to scare the cockroaches into submission. He complimented my embroidered Mexican pillows, and I wondered if he meant it sincerely before deciding that he probably did.

Conversation was difficult without the Muppets. When we talked on the phone at night I said silly, flirtatious things—a mistake that was easy to make when the room was dark and you didn't have to make eye contact. You could keep your eyes closed, the cool plastic of your phone balanced between your cheek and the pillow and the only light coming from the year-round holiday bulbs dotting the eaves of the house across the street. He chopped the mushrooms clumsily. I felt this unexpected reverse homesickness at his being in my apartment. I wished that we were finished eating, that he was catching his train and heading back to Washington, and that I could comfortably end things by phone the next day. This was probably irrational. I tried to recall if there was anything about this in my Myers-Briggs profile. I chopped the onion with robotic precision. He reached past me to get the can opener and paused to rub my back. It felt like the hand of a total stranger.

We ate the pasta on my bed while watching episodes of *The Wire* on my laptop.

"They filmed a scene in my grocery store," I told James.

"I was on the same plane as McNulty once," he said, leaning in and rasping against me with his beard. On *The Wire*, Bubbles gave an emotional speech at a Narcotics Anonymous meeting. The ziti was mush in my mouth. The mozzarella had cooled into a skin. I set it on the floor by the bed. James moved closer, put his arm around me, and gave me this smooch sort of kiss—all gums and teeth.

"It's bright in here," he said. Then he stood up and turned off all my lamps. It was us and the neighbour's Christmas lights, and I should have felt romantic. Instead, I thought of cockroaches rushing through drainpipes and silverfish slipping into electric sockets. I thought of the train that would take James back to Washington. Earlier I'd checked the schedule in eagerness at his arrival and noticed that the last train left at 11:15. When I took the plates back to the kitchen I checked the oven clock and it was already 10:30. It would take at least twenty minutes to get to Penn Station. That meant he had to leave by 10:50 to be safe.

When the episode ended he put on the next one and then settled back into place next to me. We had time for half of it, probably. He kissed me again, the brim of his hat joining our foreheads, his hand low on my back. I turned away, pretending to be invested in what was happening in the show, though I'd zoned out of several scenes and lost the thread of the story. McNulty was saying something about a serial killer. I kept thinking of the time and trying to guess how much had passed. James was cracking a topical joke, but I'd missed the beginning so I just laughed anyway. I tried to remember if he'd mentioned having a friend in Baltimore that he was planning to stay with. If he didn't, I couldn't ask him to stay at a hotel or take a several hundred dollar cab ride back, could I? And I certainly couldn't afford to offer to pay for it. Had he checked the schedule? Had he assumed he was staying here?

I knew I should just ask, so I considered how I might phrase the question: "Do you know what time your train's leaving?" or, more simply, "What time's your train leaving?" But would that seem as though I were trying to get rid of him? It wasn't really that late for a date to end.

When I checked the time again, it was 11:00. James would miss his train. When the show ended, he stretched his long arms behind him, yawning. "One more?" he asked. "Or is that enough TV for one night?"

"That might be it for me," I said. "I'm getting sleepy."

He raised his eyebrows. "It's still early, but I guess we could go to bed," he said. "I've got a morning train ride tomorrow."

I went to the bathroom and changed into my PJs, which I buttoned austerely to the neck. When I came out, James had undressed to only his boxers. We got into my bed, and I noticed how small it was for a long man whose knobbed feet angled out from under the blankets. The bed's size forced us close, a couple of spoons pressed coldly together. His beard was against the back of my neck, kissing gently. His hand roved over my hip. I made myself stay still. I impersonated taxidermy. James must have known I wasn't asleep. When his fingers passed my stomach, it was rigid.

"Be reasonable," I told myself. In the morning he'd catch his train and I'd never see him again. I could wait it out, just as I waited out my panic at the edge of Point Pleasant Park last summer, sitting on a bench facing the Atlantic, gripping the weathered seat planks on either side of me, trying to get ahead of my erratic breath. I focused on the caracara poised plumply on a branch, raising the finger-like edges of its wings.

From here it could fly to Portugal and never see a soul.

GREG BROWN

BEAR

We yawn our way through the ranger's warning.
          "Sure sure," Dilly says.
          "Got it," I say.
     Later, Dilly's disappeared and I'm staring into a tangle of tree branches and darkness.
     The stars in the night sky: glint of teeth.

The teeth are literal teeth: a grizzly bear.

Not a grizzly, it turns out: a woman inside a mechanical bear. She's studying the effects of predation on the spatial distributions of local ungulates.
     "Isn't the effect pretty obvious?" I ask.
     "We only know what we can prove," she says.

She lets me climb up and sleep beside her inside the bear, which is a pretty cozy affair for two people. No room, I mean, for a futon or kids or antique bookshelves or the other amenities that make domestic life such a rich damn joy. She insists I stick around. "Nothing serious," she says. What it is is she needs help operating the bear's haunches. "Research protocols require maximal verisimilitude," she says.

I'm mixing synthetic bear feces in a glass bowl and wondering if Assistant Professor Ursula's three-month pregnancy undermines the ongoing negotiations between the Shareholders and the Union, as we call ourselves.

"Listen," I holler through the ventilation shaft that separates the bear's two compartments. "We've grown . . . apart."

"Shh," the ventilation shaft echoes in return. "You'll wake the caribou."

"Fine. I'm going for cigarettes," I say.

"Only you can prevent forest fires," the ventilation shaft returns to me.

I'm lost, hungry, dying, dead.

That damn ranger's hovering over me, smiling to himself, some dickishness dancing on his face like *I told you so*.

ALICIA ELLIOTT

TRACKS

For the twelfth time in two days I watch as Laura shreds her vocal cords screaming and still she'll take no drugs. Her eyes are hooded with exhaustion, her hair a wet mass on her sticky forehead. It was a twenty-two-hour delivery, most of which she spent foodless and hunched over a birthing stool in the biggest suite at Tsi Non:we Ionnakeratstha Ona:grahsta. She wanted a natural delivery, she'd said. If she could feel the conception she sure as shit was going to feel the birth. That was Laura. Ever crude and to the point.

"Are you sure you don't want to go to the hosp—"

"How many times do I have to tell you? No no no no no no. No. Heck, Roy!"

The camera shrinks away. It focuses on me spitting encouragement through the pulsing crush of Laura's grip. I glimpse up at the camera—at Roy—and give a pained smile. Back then I didn't know for sure that I couldn't conceive but I had my suspicions.

I fast forward to the end, when Sherry is finally in her arms. Laura looks tired as hell, but when the camera comes for a close-up, she swats it away. "You're not allowed to catch my wrinkles on camera just because I gave birth to your kid."

There's a time lapse. When the camera starts again Laura's made up like some eager starlet. But she's not looking at the camera from beneath pristine eyelashes or blowing kisses the way she would when she was young. She's looking down at Sherry. Every touch and gesture is full of yearning, for both the present and the future. Tracing Sherry's veins with her fingers like she's following a map. Like in those small trails of blue, peeking from beneath crystalline skin, Laura saw their lives: love and anger, tenderness and humour, pain and envy. Like Laura saw their worlds—separate but interlocking: two halves of a Venn diagram.

No one watching could have seen anything but a mother and a daughter, each absolutely smitten, adoring and sizing one another up. I'm not sure I see anything different now but I continually find myself trying. Nothing ever really comes out of the blue. There must be shifting eyes somewhere in the grainy footage, a hesitation, a smile held a moment too long.

"Em." Tom is standing in the doorway in a too-big black suit. He's holding my black pumps and watching me, a question on his face. I wish he would just ask it.

"Is it time?"

He nods. I stop the video, get up, and grab my shoes.

There is a persistent, musty smell in the viewing room. It's hidden well beneath strangers' perfumes and plug-in deodorizers, but it's there. I imagine it's the smell of formaldehyde or death, though I've never really smelled either. I haven't been to a funeral since Uncle Rob's and that doesn't really count. I was so young; for all I remember I wasn't there at all. Laura said she remembered everything, from the music ("Fucking Garth Brooks") to the "huge ass mole" on the priest's chin. I didn't consider it at the time but it was strange a priest was there. Mom said when she and Uncle Rob were at the Mush Hole together, he was constantly in trouble, back-talking the priests and refusing to speak English and biting the unlucky teacher tasked with cutting his long, black Indian hair to a more "civilized" length. They beat him so he hated them; he hated them so they beat him. And yet at the end of his life a priest was praying over his Mohawk soul.

Twenty years later I'm at this funeral. Three generations—almost an entire family—gone, all put to rest courtesy of Styres Funeral Home. Laura planned her funeral shortly after she and Roy were married. It should have set off alarm bells but it didn't. At least her preparations have helped Roy. All he's had to do is nod, mute.

The room is orderly enough. Chairs arranged with absurd precision. I have the feeling that were I to take a ruler and measure the distance between each one, I'd come up with the same number every time. There must be some sort of science to grief, some manual funeral home directors adhere to, detailing the most manageable chair arrangement or flower placement for friends and family of the deceased. Everything is too calculated: the beige wallpaper, the overstuffed couches, the pre-packaged condolences.

Aunt Chelsea is at the podium, mascara that took thirty minutes of applying and re-applying to perfection now sliding, sap-like, down her cheek. Otherwise she is composed, wearing the stiff, proud pout of a once-great general facing a war tribunal. Her voice is level and dry.

"Laura was such a smart girl. Rob loved her so much. When we lost him she was four. It was . . . difficult. But she was strong."

"Smart." "Strong." Adjectives any parent could slap on the dead child they didn't care to know. I look around for evidence of skepticism. Not even a raised eyebrow. No one is thinking about Aunt Chelsea and Laura's relationship, which was tempestuous at best. In the face of death, ugly truths are redacted.

As long as I can remember, every conversation between them had notes of danger—as though any minute they'd collapse into fists and fire. I don't remember Laura ever mentioning Aunt Chelsea with anything resembling love. Even when she was six and should have still been under her mother's spell, she ignored her almost constantly, called her "Chelsea" with satisfaction.

I remember in grade nine when she was asked to prom by Mark Hanson, a white twenty-year-old senior with a car and nipple rings. She was one of the only ninth graders going— probably one of the only kids from the rez going, too—a fact she loved to remind us of, dangling it in front of our faces like a succulent piece of fruit. Laura couldn't do anything without thoroughly pissing off her mother, though, so she decided to wear Aunt Chelsea's low-cut red cocktail dress—the expensive one she bought herself in Toronto to celebrate graduating from nursing school. The way Laura told it, she sauntered home drunk at 3:00 a.m. wearing Mark's leather jacket and swinging her panties around her finger. She greeted her mother with a smile, slurring, "Guess who's a woman now?" before throwing up on the kitchen floor.

"You should've seen her face, Em," she'd said, laughing. "I've never heard her scream so loud. And all for that ugly dress! Never mind her piss-drunk daughter shooting vomit like a fucking sprinkler."

But a month after prom, when it became obvious that Mark Hanson's "gravity's as good as birth control" claim was bullshit, Aunt Chelsea didn't yell or tell her she had it coming, even if she thought it. She calmly described Laura's options, then asked what she wanted to do. When abortion was chosen, Aunt Chelsea didn't flinch or grimace in that self-satisfied way she usually did when Laura chose anything. She diligently set about doing all the work: finding a clinic, booking the appointment in Toronto, borrowing a car to drive us there. All Laura did the week before the procedure was talk about Mark. He hadn't even looked in her direction since prom.

"I'm gonna keep the fetus so I can send it to him. Like in a little jar. Oh! I should put a fake birth certificate in the bag, init? You know, like, 'Mark Hanson Jr. was aborted on this day, child to a naive girl and a small-dicked asshole.'"

"You haven't been naive since kindergarten."

"Maybe I should send it to his mom. She'd already be pissed enough an Indian snagged her son, but wouldn't it be great if she was one of those crazy pro-lifers? Like with the signs and bombs and stuff? She might actually kill Mark. Save me the trouble."

But when the day came she didn't even mention Mark. She didn't say anything at all. Afterwards, she cried against her mother's chest for almost an hour. It was strange to watch them in that embrace, as though they were any mother and daughter at any moment in history, timeless.

Laura never really mentioned the abortion to me after it happened, and out of respect for her, I never mentioned it either. I only heard her reference it once in an offhand kind of way the day Sherry was born. I didn't hear it when she said it, I must have been talking to Roy or Aunt Chelsea. It was something I noticed when I watched the video. The camera is on her bedside table. It only catches the pale curtain's flutter, but I imagine her gazing down at Sherry, maybe touching her nose with a manicured nail. Then you hear it.

"I get to keep you."

The first time I noticed it I rewound the tape to make sure that's actually what she said. Each time I heard it I felt sick. Even all those years later, on what was supposed to be one of the happiest days of her life, tragedy was playing in the background. She put on a good show but she couldn't forget. She couldn't escape. Until she did.

Maybe Laura was trying to atone for her sins. Sacrifice the child she chose for the child she didn't. Maybe that was a clue. A dot I should have connected. As though hearing those words the first time could stop the train that was, months later, barrelling forward.

Aunt Chelsea's voice has gotten thicker, the tears faster. She wobbles on her heels. Mom gets up and quietly approaches.

"It's okay, Chels." She tries to lead her away by the hand. Aunt Chelsea only clutches the podium tighter as she continues to melt into the wood. Her cries are guttural, inhuman. She knows she wasn't a good mother—the type who'd stay up all night and watch movies with Laura, or ask what she wanted to do with her life and really listen. She wasn't the type of mother a daughter would come to when terrified by her own thoughts.

Had Laura seen this, she would have offered a bemused cliché. "Better late than never." As if time is infinite and lives don't end. What good is remorse now? It might as well be never.

I lean toward Tom. "I need a cigarette." He moves to get up and I stop him quick with a shake of my head. Any time I'm alone for more than ten minutes he calls to me, or peeks his head in, or comes along with a cup of coffee or a bowl of corn soup. It's suffocating.

I stand in the doorway and inhale deeply. Freshly-shorn grass and charred hotdogs from a fundraising barbecue across the street. Evidence that other lives continue, unchanged. A slow nausea creeps up, stops short at my esophagus.

The only other person outside is a woman wearing a simple black dress. About my age. White, blond. She's whispering into her phone with her back turned. As the screen door clicks shut she turns around sharply and thrusts her phone into her purse, her eyebrows squeezed in agitation.

"Sorry." I pull out a cigarette and try to light it. My hands are shaky and imprecise.

The woman looks wary for a moment, then all creases smooth.

"It's okay. I was looking for a reason to hang up anyway."

I raise an eyebrow and she rolls her eyes.

"Ex-boyfriend," she offers.

I nod, focusing on my still-unlit cigarette. Once, twice, three times, four, and still no flame. The woman reaches into her purse, pulls out a red lighter, and flicks its head ablaze without hesitation. In a moment the end of my cigarette's aglow.

"Thanks," I say as I inhale.

"No problem."

I can feel her eyes darting back to me as she digs through her purse. I wonder what she sees. Looking in the mirror hasn't really occurred to me lately. I could have grown crow's feet overnight. My lips could have decided once and for all they were done pretending, leaving me frowning forever. I've seen other people like that. Old Mohawk women with faces like scored leather. They couldn't have always been that way. They must have been happy once, even beautiful, before some event came down on them with such unrelenting force that the smiling ended.

Laura, of course, will remain young, beautiful, tragic.

"You couldn't handle it in there, either, huh?" the woman asks.

"Nope."

She lights her own cigarette and takes a drag. Her nails are a familiar shade of pink. Showy and grossly inappropriate for a funeral.

"Viva la Vulva?"

The woman looks down at her hands and laughs. "It always sounds so much worse when said out loud like that."

"I'm not really a nail polish kind of girl." I hesitate for a moment, then puff out. "But Laura liked that one."

"Is that right? I take it you and Laura were close?"

I let the silence ring for a moment, observing her. She's too put together, too eager. I shrug. "Not really."

The woman turns in toward me. Her eyes are shrewd, calculating like a jungle cat's, her face angular and lean. Her voice drops to a whisper.

"Listen, I have a favour to ask. My name's April Hopkins and I'm a reporter for *The Star.* I know you said you didn't know Laura very well, but I could really use a few quotes. If I could just ask you a couple questions—"

"How'd you find out about this?"

She gives a thin smile. "Just a hunch."

That's bullshit. Nothing was publicized. The funeral's in downtown Ohsweken, a full hundred kilometres from where Roy and Laura lived. None of Laura's flaky friends—of which she had many—were notified. Aunt Chelsea's sticking pretty faithfully to this mourning mother routine. And Roy would never have talked to this reporter. He hasn't talked to anyone, really.

So then who was the sellout?

"I know it's probably really hard for you in light of the circumstances. But this can be your chance to set the record straight. Show people the real Laura."

Before I can even respond she pulls out a notepad and starts rifling through the pages.

"I'm going to be honest with you. A lot of people I've talked to are saying a lot of really awful things. Kayley Blatchford has gone on the record calling her a sadist. Something about getting in a lot of fights in college, really messing her knuckles up. Made it sound like a form of self-mutilation."

"Well then she obviously doesn't know the meaning of the word 'sadist,' does she? Laura got those scars in grade eight playing too much bloody knuckles."

"Really?" She fishes through her purse for a notebook and starts scribbling immediately. "Now you see why I need more opinions. It's hard to find balance with a story like this. People want a monster, so they create a monster. Especially with the whole race thing." She says it in such a careless, blasé way, the way people do when they don't have to consider the whole race thing in their everyday lives. She's right, though. I've seen it. Figures from Laura's past rematerializing in print and on tape, spinning a common tale of a troubled girl. I knew that people would talk; they did enough when she was alive. But for some reason every time another person came forward I felt attacked. Like I was the one being picked apart and analyzed.

Laura would have loved this. I can imagine her laughing, egging rumours on with some exaggerated truth or outright lie. Always building her own myth, disregarding how it affected those around her.

That doesn't explain Sherry, though. Laura was different when she had her. She prided herself on being a good mom. Took up baby massage and breastfed; I want to say something that shows this. Even something as simple as, "Laura was a fantastic mother. She loved her daughter." But I can't. Maybe the reporters and pundits are right. Maybe our family is "predisposed to violence." Maybe our people are "naturally self-destructive."

The reporter leans in closer. "Will you help me help Laura? Please?"

People begin pouring out the door. April gives only a

cursory glance to the other mourners. Her focus is me. I haven't had much experience with reporters but I can tell this woman's very good at her job. She's going to get her balanced quote—if that's what she even wants—with or without me.

I see Mom propping up Aunt Chelsea. Tom walks closely behind them, hands up, as though spotting.

I turn and grab Tom's arm. "Is it over? Where are they?"

He glances between me and April, then back toward the door. "He won't let them leave yet."

"What?"

Tom shrugs and backs away, leaving me once again with the reporter with the camera lens eyes.

"Sorry, did he just say—"

I look April straight in the face and, bluntly, as though my words were a hammer striking a nail, say, "Fuck you."

There are two matching caskets: one large, one small, both closed. There is one picture: a portrait of Laura and Sherry four months after the birth. They look so much alike. Their eyes are a matching shade of amber, their hair is smooth and straight and black. Laura refused to wear matching outfits, so their dresses clash fantastically. Both look beautiful and some-how amused, Sherry already sporting the ironic smirk it took Laura years to perfect. I want to move forward and touch the caskets but my muscles stick. I want to say something mean-ingful but nothing comes.

"What did you tell her?" Angry, accusatory. So unlike any voice I've heard I'm almost convinced I've imagined it. Then I turn and see Roy standing in the corner, his face a mass of puffy pink.

This is the first time I've seen him since the night it happened. I went straight over and saw him crumpled in a heap in the corner of Sherry's nursery, her just-used sheets ripped from her mattress and held tight against his nose. "I can still smell her." He repeated it over and over. I pulled a chair from another room and sat. It seemed wrong to sit in the rocking chair.

"What did you say to her, Em?"

I stay very still. "Who?"

"April from *The Star*."

My muscles release, slightly. "Nothing."

He exhales. "She's been following me for days trying to convince me I owe everyone a quote."

So that was how April conducted her investigative journalism: stalking. No one actually told her anything. Everyone was loyal.

"You should call the cops. Get a restraining order or something."

"No point."

I can understand why Roy hasn't talked in days. These conversations are painful, not cathartic. We're trying to talk like we normally would but it's a poor imitation. We can't even say their names. And yet by not talking about it we're still talking about it. Laura: forever the centre of attention. How she always managed to creep into conversations, even when she wasn't there, will always be a mystery to me. She was the gel in so many relationships.

Her whole relationship with Roy was the centrepiece of college gossip. Before Roy, all of Laura's flings were interchangeable. Big, sturdy barrels of men with stamina and little else. The closest she ever came to loving a boy was drunkenly tattooing a high school boyfriend's name on her shoulder after graduation. She never bothered to cover it after they broke up.

Roy was something else altogether. He was the quiet, studious roommate of some moron she was dating in college. The night Laura met Roy, Bryan drank three pitchers of beer by himself. On their way back to his apartment he collapsed. She dragged his two-hundred-and-thirty-pound frame to the door, swearing and grunting the whole time. As she rifled through his pockets for keys, Roy opened the door: wiry, pale, freckled. Between the two of them, they managed to get Bryan inside. Then Roy offered to make Laura a French press of coffee. And that's when she said she knew.

"Not once did he look down my shirt. And I was wearing my black tank top—you know, the one with the sequins? Cleavage everywhere, and here he is, asking me my opinions on Akira Kurosawa. Like he actually thought a rez girl like me would know anything about Akira Fucking Kurosawa."

She seemed amazed that there was a man alive who would want to spend four hours talking to her without the promise of sex. That there was a man alive who could see her as a person.

I'm not sure he did, though. Roy marrying Laura was like the nerd finally bagging the head cheerleader. For all his reverence for her, I think Roy both recognized and relished this. It was almost grotesque the way they showed one another off: he with his gorgeous, glowing Pocahottie, she with her white, sure-to-earn-six-figures sugar daddy.

When they announced their engagement six months later it was met with hard cynicism. Typical Laura, everyone back home thought, riding a whim to get attention. I thought so, too, until their wedding day. We were in the back room waiting for our cue to leave, she in her white gown. She turned to me, her face pursed.

"Em. What if he finally realizes he's marrying me and just leaves?"

Their marriage was more than an impulse. It was a dive into the dark and she was terrified.

And yet she left him, willingly, taking everything with her.

I reach over, feel the crisp linen of Roy's sleeve—

"Don't." He brushes my hand off. It was stupid of me to think he could handle these kinds of interactions. I can't even imagine how he could get dressed, much less put up with condolences from strangers. I try to get him to look into my face but he won't.

"These past few days all I could think about was talking to you. I had a list of questions. A whole goddamn speech. But now that you're in front of me . . ."

"Maybe this isn't the right time for this," I say. Roy rubs his hands over his face. I feel a numbness creeping up my knees. I shouldn't have worn such high heels.

"I don't want you there. It doesn't seem right."

For a moment the room seems to tilt.

"What do you mean? You don't want me where?"

He blinks and blinks.

"You don't want me where, Roy?"

"The burial. The reception after. I didn't really want you here, but you're her cousin. Her best friend. People would ask questions."

"But . . . nothing happened."

Roy looks inflamed. Sharp words are waiting to be said, I can tell. I hope he says them. I hope they draw blood. There's been enough pretending for the sake of saving face. We did what we were supposed to. All the tiptoeing, the planning . . . all of it was for nothing. I never got to taste second-hand red wine on his tongue or feel his slender fingers between my thighs. I never will. I shouldn't feel resentment—not now, of all times—and yet here it is, crippling and noxious.

He looks directly at me and his face is set. "Please. Don't. Come."

Every five to ten minutes the high-pitched shriek sounds. The wheels are stopped by force. Violent, desperate, like the last moment of struggle before surrender. The subway train smashes to a halt: doors open, people rush, bells chime, doors close. The station left barren.

With traffic it took me two and a half hours to drive here, ten minutes to find parking. St. George. One of the busiest subway stations in Toronto. Isolating even at capacity. It's a depressing shade of green—one I imagine I'd find peeling from the walls of a crack house bathroom on the Trail.

I lean out, well past the platform's yellow line. When I turn back eyes are on me, some wide and worried, some dull and uncaring. People watch and watch but never do anything.

It happened here, at the centre of two lines. A crossroad, of sorts. Was that intentional? I know I need to stop. There's no meaning in these walls or their placement on a map. Only she knows why she chose this place, if it was even a choice at all.

No two accounts are the same, but all agree she wheeled Sherry off the elevator in that obscenely expensive stroller she loved so much. Either she didn't say anything or she cooed to Sherry as she moved to the end of the platform. The train going Northbound wailed its way into the station. Sherry started to cry. Laura picked her up and clutched her to her chest, kissing her or trying to shush her or looking maudlin. The air started to shift, another whistling could be heard.

The TV screen said the next train Southbound would be arriving in less than a minute. Some people thought she was just peeking down the tunnel to see the train, the way people do. Others said she looked distraught. At the last minute she shifted Sherry onto her hip as she took off her purse and thrust it into the seat of the stroller. Or she wasn't wearing a purse. Then she turned her back toward the oncoming train, hugged Sherry tight, and stepped sideways off the platform.

I didn't notice her unhappiness. I was too busy parcelling pieces of her perfect life to take for myself. She practically told me her plans right there on the phone and I hung up. Hung up to meet her husband in Burlington—the halfway point between our homes, our families. Back then, of course, I told myself it wasn't cheating. It was easy enough to believe; our skin barely touched. When it did, though, those slight, soft strokes were everything to me. Amazing that something so small could be so erotic. I lived for the chance that we'd brush hands under the table. Even as it was happening to me I put myself above it. Roy and I were doing things the right way. We were going to keep collateral damage to a minimum.

That last time we talked Laura was going on about Sue Stevenson, soon to be Sue Kristoff. She had just sent Laura an invitation to her wedding and Laura was micro-analyzing the handwritten postscript. Apparently "Vlad and I would love for you to come. We have so much catching up to do!" was code for "I married someone richer and want to rub it in your face."

"Maybe she really does want to see you and catch up. She was your roommate. You guys were close."

"We were not. Sue and all those white, trust fund bitches don't make friends. They gather audiences. I could call every one of them right now and tell them I'm going to kill myself and they'd just laugh and ramble on about how they used to cut themselves in eighth grade."

I laughed, the way I always did.

"I'm serious. And it's really fucking sad when you think about it."

"Look, I got to go. I'm supposed to meet Tom for dinner in ten. We can trash all your old friends tomorrow. I'll call you around, say, four?"

"Oh. Okay. Emily?"

"Yeah?"

Something big was bothering her. She never used my full name. I could hear her ragged breathing as I feverously applied red lipstick in front of the bathroom mirror.

"Speak now or forever hold your peace." I meant for it to be playful.

"Forget it. I'll talk to you tomorrow."

I don't remember what I ate for dinner that night, what I wore, what lie I told Tom to get out of the house. I don't remember anything that Roy and I talked about. But I remember the hollow of her voice, or at least I tell myself I do.

JASON JOBIN

BEFORE HE LEFT

The next morning when I crawled from bed and peeked out the window, Billy still sat below the tree. Sat as if tranquilized, legs in lotus, nestled in the curved roots of our front yard's cedar. Maybe we needed the authorities. Child Services. A babysitter with the new rhetoric. Some wise, jean-vested mentor. They'd have so many questions. Craig unwound himself from the covers and came to stand with me. He had brown ingots of mucus at the inner corner of his eyes, hair in spikes, the look of someone whose shoulders are harnessed in backpack straps. Open-mouthed, we watched our son from the bedroom window. Billy's posture hadn't changed since the previous night. The grey blanket had fallen or been shrugged off his shoulders. Songbirds hopped around him and pecked at the grass and I wondered what their claws must feel like and if he noticed them.

"What do we do?" I sucked on the hair in my mouth.

Craig smelled like weeks without laundry.

"I checked earlier, like 4 a.m. He didn't touch the toast I brought out. Squirrels ate most of it." He squinted and picked at the shoulder of his white T-shirt.

"How do you know it was squirrels?"

"It was torn to shreds, covered in fur."

"You can't assume and just—"

"Jan. Jan." He put his arm around me, dug a few fingers into the side of my breast. "It's okay. He'll give up eventually."

"That's what I'm worried about."

We let that sink in. Wind now rippled Billy's short hair. I pressed into Craig's ribs. He felt heavy next to me, waterlogged.

"He needs to stay hydrated," I said.

"He needs a rain tarp," said Craig.

"Maybe a protein bar."

"What's the forecast?"

"I don't know, I don't know. Rain and downpours and—"

"We can set up a tarp." Craig nodded seriously at the idea of tarps.

"But it's cold out there; it's so cold. Freezing out there. Frost on his eyelashes."

"Jan, we can get him some warm clothes and a space heater. One of those restaurant patio lamps."

"The lamps that shoot fire?"

"Yeah. The ones with warnings."

"One of those big red poles that get so hot and look like a machine gun."

"Yeah."

We were fine. Solutions had arisen.

"We can't do this," I said. "We need to stop."

"Stop?"

"We can't be okay with, can't facilitate, this."

"He's out there under a tree, Jan. That's where we are."

It all started with the dragonfly, is how I chart the timeline. You can't make sense of something without a timeline. Billy was eight, I think. Around when Craig had admitted to getting a drink after work with a female colleague and when I began going to the gym five days a week. Around that time. And maybe because of the working out, or maybe because of an invisible lead collar I felt around my neck, a heavy, bruising leash, I stayed perpetually exhausted.

Craig had gone downtown to watch a hockey game, I hoped and prayed, while Billy and I tidied up dinner. Billy stood barefoot on a small plastic stool in front of our triple sink. I'd been leaning against the window in the kitchen nook, my cheek flush with the glass. Songbirds flew big sorties over the yard. Fork tines rang off spoons and other forks. Spears of twilight transformed our dusty kitchen into some glossy Le Creuset ancient tomb. I tried to keep awake in that haze of noise and light.

I was coming off a day filled with box squats and jackknives and the one where you swing ropes like they've bitten your hands and you must shake them off before you die. I hurt all over.

Billy hummed behind me as the sink filled—low note, low note, high note. His hum changed intensity every few seconds. *Hm, hmm, hmmmmm.* Melodic trills, weird, jarring bursts. Adventure music. He punched the water and spritzed it at himself. He hummed, whistled, drummed the taps. He'd sometimes smear bubbles on his chin and, thus bearded, cast spells.

I soaked in his noises. My eyelids warmed in the light.

A strange slosh from the sink brought me back.

I turned around to see Billy standing weirdly upright by the bay window. He'd left the tap on, oblivious to the bright sheet of water connecting sink and floor.

He had a dragonfly's severed head between two fingers, held up to his eye like a jewel.

I ran and shut off the tap. Stood there dumbly as my socks took on water, too tired to connect any dots.

A dragonfly had gotten caught in our glue trap. I didn't say anything and began to spread towels. I mopped what I could. Billy just stood at that window the whole time and for some reason I still didn't say anything. Finally I went and stood behind him. I asked, *What are you doing?* He said, *I had to kill it.* He told me how he couldn't get the bug loose from the glue strip, even though it was only caught by a single wing. Every time he tried to pry the wing loose, the dragonfly's three other wings would buzz at the touch of his finger, and one would catch in the glue, and when he'd try to pry that wing loose, again all the other wings would buzz and another would get stuck. Around and around. He said it would have starved to death anyway.

Out in public, I'd feel Billy near me. *Feel* him, like palpably feel something, I don't know what, emanating off him in staggered, gentle waves that didn't quite prickle, but you imagined they might soon or could. And I'd tell him, Billy, if you open one more chakra outside the house I'm going to take away all your sitting cushions. He did that sometimes, open them in public. At first, I didn't sense much beyond a faint ripple at the periphery of his body's outline, or that my head would swivel toward him one moment before he actually entered a room I was in. But as he got deeper into it, really harnessing and accessing the Tall Energies, as he would describe them, the sensation became something almost impossible to keep secret, felt like those fine Velcro brushes across your skin. He'd do it in Bed Bath & Beyond, at school, even visiting the dentist. Super-crowded places. The mall. I'd say, Billy, if you even tickle or remotely touch your heart chakra in the food court, I'm going to take away every single one of your bronze chiming bowls, so help me God, I'll put them in the top cupboard. Sometimes he'd relent, but sometimes he'd zoom through his heart chakra to throat to third eye, causing heads to swivel en masse in our general direction as people tried to figure out what was happening.

We'd find Billy sitting in the yard or in the nooks and crannies of the house. I'd look for his short, sandy hair against the backdrop of fence, lawn, apple tree. He had cheeks like little buns. A big forehead (mine). This cute pointy chin. A small boy.

He didn't always sit in lotus. Sometimes he'd be in a regular cross-legged pose or have both legs straight out in front of him. On his head one day, all fours the next, then in some kind of twisted sideways sprawl. He sat so still for so long. My Billy, now a monk, now a garden gnome.

He'd collected several Buddhist texts by then, been reading and studying them for who knows how long before we exposed him. *Pali Canon, Taisho Tripitaka, Tibetan Kangyur,* and various leather-bound Mahayana Sutras, some books without titles or, seemingly, any text in them whatsoever, though he'd dodge questions regarding those.

Schoolwork hit a wall. I'd find abandoned math sheets in his dresser, geography assignments under his bed, writing prompts folded into orchids on his windowsill. Dust-caked geometry sets and cartons of colouring pencils still in their Staples bags piled up behind his bedroom door. Paperless binders. A copy of *The Little Prince* eight months overdue from the library with spirals drawn over every mention of the moon. Notebooks of blank pages with maybe one circle drawn on the last page and the caption *Oh*. I'd walk by his room, ask: What did you learn today? Always he'd reply: *Don't worry*.

Teachers called the house, their voice a half whisper. They weren't sure if he'd spoken a single word in class all term. Could we test him for autism? Could we get a doctor to prescribe amphetamines? Had they prescribed too many amphetamines? Was he vaccinated?

Craig maybe had it worse than me. This was his boy. His son. The one who would become him, beat him at sports when it was finally appropriate, fight tigers, arm wrestle lightning. Billy cradled grasshoppers like newborns. Severed branches, errant spiders, road-killed birds on the boulevard—all might feel his love. One day he sat for hours with a dead, emerald green hummingbird shrined in his lap. When I looked for it later on, I couldn't find the bird's body anywhere, nor see any disturbed plots of grass or overturned soil. But I was too afraid to ask him about it, figured boys will be boys with corpses.

I tracked down a local Buddhist monk through Craigslist. He called himself Ashwa. Two days later, Ashwa showed up on our doorstep looking so smooth-faced and ambiguously ethnic that I wanted to cry.

I let him in the house without saying anything. Ashwa wore a sort of red sarong that went to his ankles. I couldn't tell how the sarong actually stayed on his thin body: there were no knots, clips, or belts of any sort. Ashwa was bald. Maybe thirties or forties. Threadbare sandals. Ginger-root toes, the skin a dark, scabby brown. I wanted to kneel there, Pope-like, debased—Mom had always termed it *humility*—and clean his feet.

I remember how he closed the door behind himself and waited without even the vague suggestion of fidgeting. Water peppered the glass door panels. The sounds of wind and creaking trees, our fence a constant wooden groan. It had rained for three days.

"Mrs. Baker," he said.

"Thank you for coming." I bowed without thinking.

He only smiled and didn't bow back. "So, your son is pursuing enlightenment?"

"Would you be able to talk with him?"

"How do you mean?"

"I don't know. Talk to him, explain that he's a kid and needs to realize that he's just a kid and has to live a bit and do things and speak to people."

Ashwa considered this. "Is he here?"

"He's upstairs to the right, in his room. We have tried everything."

Ashwa slipped out of his sandals and walked by me up the stairs. His feet crunched against the wood. The edge of his shoulder blades stuck through the back of his tunic like the stumps of fallen trees.

I sat in the kitchen with the lights off, one fingernail picking at the kitchen table's lacquer. Some kind of resin. Expensive. Three layers. Was it okay to have this man upstairs with Billy? I hadn't let Craig know yet, didn't want him to worry or over-think. Rain curled down the windows in invisible channels, paths left by Windex, pollen, the oily footprints of flies. The greens of the lawn, the ash of the sky. Our cedar tree, beads of water on every twig and needle. The patio chimes rang crazily.

Eventually, I stood from the chair and crept upstairs, stop-ping short of Billy's room. I tried to get my head as close to the edge of the door as I could, one ear almost on the ground.

"—and so," said Billy in his clear but uneven voice, "envi-sion a sphere, like the world, filled with dirt. Really picture this sphere, its curved, complete surface, its weight. Let all the things other than the sphere fade, they are gone, now there is only the sphere of dirt, hanging in grey. After that becomes comfortable in your mind, let the dirt also disappear. The sphere is just hollow now, transparent. Do you see it? Finally, let the sphere itself go. See how it fades. There is nothing. Allow it to go. This is no—"

"*Okay*," I said, half falling into the room. I crouched there with my fingernails in the floor. "That's about enough."

They both turned to me from where they sat facing each other.

"I understand this may not have been your goal, Mom," said Billy with a small nod.

"Ashwa, you can go."

Ashwa bowed to Billy, I swear to God. He started walking out, but paused as he passed me.

"Would it be possible to return at a later date?" he asked.

"Fuck no," I whispered to him.

"Mom, this is unnecessary. He's well-intentioned."

"You need to do your math homework and make your bed."

Billy nodded.

I noticed Ashwa had left. The faint closing of the front door downstairs.

"He was very wise," said Billy, his eyes on the crenulations in the ceiling drywall.

"Dinner is at six."

Billy turned eleven and Leandra, a girl who lived down the street, came over to play. They set up in the backyard and began to dig a hole. I watched them from the kitchen. Clouds sped by overhead, their shadows like big swollen birds. I'd hoped for some profound connection, a bridge for Billy back to Regular Land. The kids hardly spoke. Leandra might say something, smile, then lapse back into digging. They dug for probably two hours. Such focused excavation. Crouched quite close to one another, their hips and elbows occasionally touching. I'd forced Billy to wear a white T-shirt along with his loose yellow pants. He still would not wear shoes or socks. Leandra wore a pretty flowered sun dress. Her black hair hung as if decorated with heavy beads. They each dug with a small garden trowel. Eventually they stopped digging and stared into the hole for several minutes and I couldn't see their lips to know if they spoke. Sweat shone off their necks. Their shoulders rose and fell and I thought: baby camels, baby camels. And then Leandra twisted to the side and kissed Billy on the cheek. Said something. Billy backed away, almost in a hop, but stayed crouching with his fingers in the grass. Said something. Leandra's face softened, caved in. She unwound from her squat and walked from the yard, waved at Billy without looking back. That wave. Billy stayed crouched next to the hole. He peered into the hole, then at the red gate she'd left through, then back into the hole. Billy's sun-cast shadow a long thin spear by then, the day gone a shade of amber. He crouched there for some time. I couldn't look away. I noticed muscles in his cheek for the first time, crimped lines in his upper lip. Mastication. Rapid blinks like his face might be able to fly away. I was rapt. Guilty and rapt, my chest hot. Billy crouched by that hole until the clouds slowed and thickened to steel wool overhead and I made him come inside.

One day we finally managed to get Billy down to the ocean on a family outing. Craig seemed like the odd one out for once, claiming back pain, and said he'd rather sit inside and stay cool and have a beer. Billy had quietly agreed to come when I, after some searching, found him in the downstairs den sitting beside the couch with his fingers arranged into a complex triangle. This was summer and the absence of school had been good.

We drove to Dallas Road. Craig parked in the shade below a bright orange arbutus. I peeled my bare legs off the car's seat and stretched and made sure we didn't forget our small cooler with the turkey sandwiches. Billy wore only his billowy yellow pants, no shoes or socks or T-shirt, the day hot enough for legitimate fashion-minimalism.

We didn't lay out a blanket. Too much driftwood and rock cluttered the shore. Each of us found a comfortable nook between uprooted trunks or stones and settled in to watch the ocean. Gulls swooped above a quartet of paragliders. Gusts and white waves throwing themselves about in the distance.

Quiet on the shore. Our sheltered cove with its hot air and driftwood stacked as if thrown. All felt slow and viscous.

Billy had chosen a hollowed volcanic bowl, a dry tidal pool maybe, and sat cross-legged in the depression and looked very small and like he was held in an immense cupped palm. He stared at the paragliders as they took off from the water, landed, took off again. Though he didn't himself participate in sports or games anymore, he'd often stare at people doing these things.

I went over to where Billy sat and dropped into a deep squat next to the stony depression.

"How's it going?" I said.

"Good."

"I love you."

His eyebrows moved but he didn't respond.

"You love me too, right?"

"It's been bothering you, yes?"

"What's been bothering me?"

"I do love you, of course." He brought one knee to his chest.

"And do you love this beach?"

"Of course."

"And that guy over there with the blue shirt?"

"Yes."

"These things are different, Billy. I'm your mother."

"Attachment to these things, Mom, that's where we get caught up. That kind of love brings so much pain."

"That kind of love? You mean like mine and your dad's?"

A nod.

"We all have difficult moments, but we are happy with our love."

"That type of love is about 'me,' about 'I.'"

"Do you not want that?"

"The kids in my class fight and scheme and send notes. Penny kissed Isaac behind Gerald's back and they all don't speak to each other anymore. I saw Gerald sitting by himself on a swing hardly swinging at all. Barely moving."

"That's just a part of growing up, honey."

I ran my fingers through sand. A spider appeared, skittered under a log.

"What were you like as a child?" he said.

Some grits of sand clung to the ridge of his right cheek. I resisted the urge to brush them off.

"I was just a regular girl," I said.

"What does that mean?"

"I sometimes, you know, kissed people, and I sometimes sat on swings and was sad and hardly swinging at all."

"What made you the most sad as a kid?"

"Oh, I don't remember."

Both of us stared at the deep black-blue of the ocean. Snow-fall of white foam past the point. Closer in, the water bulged with a strange flatness, taut sheets over a sleeping animal.

"I remember being sad when I was excluded," I said.

"Why were you excluded?" Billy had a way of asking questions that made you realize you could legitimately say anything, no matter how vile.

"I wasn't always excluded. Only sometimes. There was this group of girls. The group had a name, but I can't remember the name. Someone had invented a name and everyone else was too scared to question it. I was a little fat back then. Chubby. The most popular girl was a really skinny girl named Madeleine, with black hair and the tiniest wrists you've ever seen."

Billy only nodded.

"She'd always put things around her tiny wrists and exclaim how it was much too big for *her wrists* and would only fall off. She'd force kids to give her their watches and bracelets. To try on. This was back when people had watches and bracelets."

Billy's eyes were perfect ovals.

I don't know that I'd ever told anyone this.

"Sometimes, I'd be in the group and we'd be mean to other people, and sometimes I'd be out of the group and they would be mean to me. Always one way or the other and I couldn't figure it out."

I could still hear the other girls call me fat, their teeth visible, how they closed up like a culvert of human backs. I'd stare at their ring of giggling bodies from wherever off to the side I'd chosen to stand during my exile. The feeling of being a paused television. Not able to leave. Not able to join. Tent pegs through my feet. I never cried when they did that. Always felt that the world meant for it to happen and that maybe the sky would splinter and fall on the other girls in big, jagged shards, fall on them till the only things left were little pink hair ties and candy necklaces and thick, frilled socks and I'd sort of tiptoe through the wreckage putting everything in a big canvas sack.

Two weeks later, Billy sat down next to the tree in our front yard and would not come in when I yelled that lunch was ready. At first, Craig and I laughed at the spectacle, nodded knowingly like *Wait until an ant crawls on his toe.* Then we went more neutral, certain he'd come in by nightfall. By midnight for sure. Soon we pleaded and argued and threatened to carry him bodily into the house. I could say we should have just picked him up. Got Craig to cradle him like the victim of a house fire. There was a moment, both of us knelt right in front of Billy, and I could really feel the softness of the soil and grass against my knees, where Craig and I looked at each other with a kind of *So, are we going to do this? Can we do this?* intention, and neither of us made the signal to pull the trigger. We both, I'm sure, knew that this was the time to slip an arm under his little knees and back and swoop him inside. Neither of us gave the signal. The wetness of the grass began to soak through my tights. Cool air tickled my earlobes, seemed to hold them gently. Craig went in the house and came out with a grey moving blanket. He draped the blanket around Billy's shoulders. Billy didn't move. So still. Head slightly bowed, legs in full lotus, the sole of his right foot pointed at the stars.

"We're going to go in now, Billy," I said. "We love you, you should join us."

"Let us know if you need anything," said Craig. "I'll bring some food out in a few hours."

On the second day, Craig called in sick to work. I skipped the gym. Billy didn't move as we strung a holey blue camping tarp over where he sat. Craig suspended one of his hydration bladders from a branch. We angled the drinking hose to hang down near Billy's unmoving mouth. I placed a chocolate mint Cliff Bar (with the package torn half open) on the grass next to Billy's pale little right hand. We both sat in front of Billy for about twenty minutes, seeking communion, awaiting his response, like it was owed, before we gave up and went inside for a glass of wine.

Mid-afternoon, there came a knock on the door. It was Ashwa, now wearing a darker, more fuchsia, sarong. The same unnerving smoothness coated his features.

"What do you want?" I said.

"I, well, my order—our temple is downtown, off Johnson, near the pagoda—wishes to see your son."

He stood, half bent it seemed, but also poised. His face appeared so hairless, laser-depilated, a stranger to beards. Each pore a little pocket of shiny skin.

"I told you to leave us alone."

"I understand your desire for privacy. We've been occasionally passing by to perhaps see him and—"

"You've been watching us?"

"Oh no, no, no. Not watching. Occasionally passing by to perhaps catch a glimpse or speak—"

"You've been *watching us*?"

"Who is it?" yelled Craig from the kitchen. I heard wine being poured into a glass.

I didn't say anything for a few seconds. Ashwa somehow maintained eye contact and did not. He kept his gaze on the shark-tooth outer edge of my left eye.

"Who is it, Jan?" yelled Craig again.

"Ashwa," I said, though not to Craig.

He nodded.

"Billy has gone out into the yard and sat down below our tree and refuses to speak or move."

"Below the cedar tree."

"Yes, below the cedar tree. Is that somehow significant?"

"I do not know."

"It's the only species of tree in our yard."

"I see," he said.

"What exactly is he doing?"

"I do not know."

"Well, I know he's meditating. I know. But what is he doing?"

"May I come in?"

I moved aside, and he stepped into the house, his sarong rustling past the door frame. For some reason, we began to walk down the hall, away from Craig and the kitchen.

"Janet, it's likely Billy is progressing to a deeper period of reflection, a more profound awakening."

We passed the laundry room. I felt the weight of my body on each socked foot.

"How profound?" I asked.

"Who can say? Great teachers often seclude themselves for very long periods of time."

"He's just a kid."

"In one sense, yes."

"What other senses are there?"

"Who can say?"

"That's cute. He isn't eating."

Ashwa nodded.

"He hasn't had anything to drink, or slept, in two days."

Ashwa nodded.

We had by then circumnavigated the main floor's maze of hallways and entered the kitchen. Craig, wineglass poised against his bottom lip, froze as we walked by. He tracked our passing with his eyes. Ashwa at my side in his sandals and purple dress, me pretending like Craig knew what was happening. I shrugged and kept focused on my feet. We kept walking and eventually stopped at the sliding-glass doors to the yard. Billy hadn't moved. Our contraptions of food and water dangled around him under the tarp looking very DIY and embarrassing.

Ashwa peered through the glass at Billy. I noticed the flare of his nostrils as he breathed. They seemed to pull up instead of to the side.

"He should probably take water," said Ashwa.

"We set up water."

"It should be poured into his mouth from a chalice. I can do it."

"I don't know."

"Might I go sit with him?"

I slumped. "Sure."

Ashwa eased open the door and stepped lightly down to the half-wet grass. His sandals made a soft squishing noise as he approached Billy. He knelt before Billy and put his hands together, with two fingers pointed forward, like a kid pretending to fire a gun. And that was that. He didn't pull out a chalice and give Billy water. Nor did he attempt to say anything. I watched him for several minutes, tried to see any potential arcing lines of spiritual energy, the crackle in the air, but nothing happened. Back inside, I told Craig about the visitor. Soon I went upstairs and lay on my bed overtop of the blankets despite my shivering in the clammy house. I slept for hours and woke in darkness with spit down the side of my face, eyes heavy as stones, the feeling that so much had gone on in my absence. Upon going downstairs, I could see Ashwa and Billy by the patio lamps, unmoved, like I hadn't slept at all and only turned down the volume to some negative number.

After first thinking he'd run off and given up, I found Craig in the garage cleaning his Lexus. He'd somehow found the vacuum cleaner and looked to be sucking dust out of the coffee holder with the fabric cleaning attachment. On the ground around the vehicle lay a spread of Chamois cloths, Armor All, paper towels, car polish, an old toothbrush, newly shiny black floormats, and a pile of quarters and crumpled bills.

"Gotta take care of business," he said, before ducking back into the backseat.

I left him to it and went to sit on the floor of the laundry room with my back against the dryer.

Three days passed. We called in for food. Craig had finished cleaning every component of his car by then, after which he slept for fifteen hours. Beyond that he'd been sitting in the den with his nose in his childhood photo albums and boxes of sports medals. He leafed through old school binders and Duo-Tangs. I had no idea the sheer amount of paper he'd hoarded. Boxes I'd never seen or moved or had to organize at his behest. Where had he kept them?

At some point on the third day Ashwa was able to pour water into Billy's mouth from a stone bowl covered in sigils that I think may have just been musical notes. The weather dipped into rain and wind. Gusts lashed at Billy's overhead tarp, sent our hydration bladder's hose whipping around like an angry cobra in the dark. But Billy did not move. Ashwa stayed out there with him through it all. I swear at some point, from my bedroom window's vantage—I'd been spending more of my time there, skipping the gym to watch him; at regular intervals, I'd drop to the floor and do push-ups, sit-ups, burpees, leg raises, pistol squats—I saw Billy's lips move as Ashwa kneeled very close in front of him. Swore that Ashwa's lips also moved.

After seeing this ghostly whisper between the two of them, I began to jump rope. My rope was red and had long ago ceased to hurt when it struck my shins. The *thwaps* came faster and faster, echoed around the bedroom. It got warm. Little Rorschachs of sweat painted the floor under my feet. Billy would not stop me jumping. Billy would know I was up there. Thirty minutes in I could hardly stand but I kept on. Forty minutes. Fifty. Had I always been jumping? Was there other than this?

Through this all, Billy didn't budge from his position below the tree. Sweat pooled in my navel, the small of my back, the shelves of my ribs. Dark blotches of it spread over the front of my sweatpants between my legs, I knew, I just knew without looking, crept like melanomas through the grey cotton. My feet swelled, went soft and sticky. And then I stopped, though it felt like I kept jumping. The room shuddered up and down. I tried to breathe. I took up the jump rope and swung it against the floor like a whip. Again, again. I drew long welts in the hardwood. Next, the jade plant on the window sill. It shattered and broke over the floor. Chips of clay and soil flying. I turned to the wall and I swung and swung until shreds of daisy wallpaper hung in the air and billowed around me and stuck to my wet arms like Band-Aids. This swinging much more tiring than the jumping. Dirt and wallpaper in my eyes, my mouth. The room a bizarre aquarium. I made for the door, the stairs, Billy. We had to talk. My legs went out at the top of them. Down I went. I'd never before thought so much about the edge of each individual stair, how they are rectangular, where they would be when I encountered them, how each one might caress my back or arm or ankle. I came to a stop at the first landing, half upside down, one eye either swollen shut or held in a spastic wink I could not calm.

Craig found me there and didn't say anything. He scooped me up, but I made him put me down. Told him I was fine. A little accident was all. He pretended to believe me and it made me feel better. I paced around the house trying not to limp and eventually excused myself to the bathroom and cleaned my face in the sink, scraped off as much of the plant and clay and paper residue as I feasibly could without showering. Then I sat in the living room and looked out the window specifically from an angle where Billy under the tree was not in my line of sight. Just our regular yard. Our flimsy blue fence. The depressions in the grass we'd never been able to make flat.

On the fourth day, Billy was gone. All the contraptions we'd set up around him were still there, but Billy, who had been at the centre of it all, had vanished. I didn't wake up Craig for some reason. He lay in bed folded around one of our thick down pillows, clutching it tightly to his nose. I padded from the room barefoot, down the stairs, out the patio doors to the wet lawn. I walked to where Billy had been, the patch of grass he'd been sitting on more green than anywhere else. I touched the grass where he'd sat. The blades bent under my fingers and I swear I could almost hear them flex. Grass like in spring. Warm to the touch. I looked around for Ashwa, but there was no sign of him either. No monks watched me from across the street. No one in a sarong visible anywhere. Sunlight peeked through thin strips of cloud over the city. I felt around the tree, sank my hands into the mud near the roots, traced my fingers up the bark, the soft bubbles of sap. Perhaps Billy was camouflaged, watching me. A test. Maybe he'd gone inside to sleep in his room, though I knew that wasn't the case, knew that his blanket would be as severely tucked into the bed frame as it had been for the last week, not a wrinkle in the cotton, tight as skin.

I tried to feel him, the way I'd felt him when he put off the vibrations that first time in the mall food court as we lined up to buy cheeseburgers. Felt only the cold wind, the rub of my tank top against my breasts, the wet ankles of my pyjama bottoms. Where was he. Where was he. Where was he. He'd buried himself underground. Was at this very moment look- ing up at me through a hole in the network of roots and plant skeletons. He'd taken refuge inside the tree, folded the wood around himself like a gnarled quilt. How would I get him out? With an axe? With lightning? He'd shrunk himself to the size of a bean to live in the foundations of the house. To live with the dust mites and spiders. Gone invisible. Or walked up the street with Ashwa and his monks, the purple brigade. Walked up the street in absolute silence in the dark of night, the streetlights having failed or been quelled by a giant thumb. Walked and walked and felt no pain in his little bare feet. Gone up the street to the big water with the driftwood flung into piles like anti-tank hedgehogs from the Second World War. Watched the waves. But not stayed there. Kept going. Walked to a small, planked room with pillars like the legs of elephants. Made a little home there and served cups of tea to his guests. Spoke in low tones to the other monks and they all understood what he wanted and it was all very simple and he'd be back by the weekend for a good casserole, cheese bubbling over the sides. We'd sit in the cool sun, the monks too, the neighbours, but not under the tree and in real chairs, and he'd say something like I want to be a travel agent, a whale biologist, a karate master, and that's how it would turn out.

SOFIA MOSTAGHIMI

DESPERADA

After Shanghai, I caught a cheap flight to Bangkok. In the sky, I met a group of Australians who joked about North Korea and Kim Jong-il the whole time and who said, "G'day, mate" for my pleasure. We parted ways at the airport, then I travelled to Ko Phangan, where I think I was roofied at the Full Moon Party. Good strangers took pity on me, and one of them reminded me of Kimia. This is what the group of girls told me later at breakfast, on the beach, pretty girls, sticky already with the 9 a.m. humidity. I saw now that the girl sitting across our small, square table looked nothing like my little sister. But when she smiled so gracious-like and thoughtfully, that was when I noticed it.

"You gave me tons of life advice," she said, with that inno-cent, fearless tone only nineteen-year-olds have. "We're from Vancouver, by the way," she added. "You're Canadian too, right? You said washroom yesterday instead of bathroom." Her voice had that bright, elastic West Coast warmth.

"From Toronto," I said.

"You also said that all that putting my career first was extremist feminist bullshit."

They were like words rising from a grave that hadn't been dug for me yet.

"I said what?"

"And you said, strangers are only scary if you're someone to fear. You said that, like, um, what did she say again?"

She'd turned to the others, who were blank and beautiful and worthy of love—I thought, why did I ever leave my city? These people exist where I'm from too.

"She said that, like, people are only scared of other people if they're, like, fixating on some evil part of themselves."

"I did?"

"You're wise as fuck," the third one said. The fourth one stayed silent in my presence, and the other girls made fun of her for it. She didn't care. She'd keep staring at me only with these black eyes.

"My sister, by the way," I finally told them. "The one you reminded me of, Kimia. That was her name. She's dead." I needed to see their faces when I said it. I needed it the way I need to be fucked by strangers. But why?—I thought of him, and how his ears must have burned.

"Oh my God."

"I am so sorry."

"We're so sorry."

"Oh my God, so sorry," they said.

They were young, and so sweet. They travelled with their parents' money and had bodies that bended with confidence in strange lands, that spoke of such perfect, disgraceful privilege—and yet their smiles were not to be mistaken for empathy.

"I'm kidding," I said. I couldn't cling to the truth. I didn't want to. "My sister almost died. But she's alive," I said. I lied. But the key to lying is to latch on to that idea as if it were the only fact in this world worth knowing.

I stayed with them a while longer. I learned that all four of them were trained Yoga instructors. They were travelling to India next, for further certification, but had decided to stop first in Thailand.

"The food is amazing here. Have you tried the stir-fried noodles?" they asked.

Which was when I thought of that famous novel-turned-movie about eating and travelling, which was when I thought of how food had not been a concern of mine, not once on this trip, and then I thought of the last supper that I had enjoyed.

My whole life, I told them, after a few more beers, my whole life, has been a giant sacrifice.

"For who?" one or all of them had asked.

"To who, you mean."

"To *whom*."

"To whom?"

"To life."

They laughed. I laughed too, but by then my soul felt like wine. Like I had turned water to wine, and that's the opposite of it all, isn't it? Why did he do that? Why did I know a story that did not even belong to my people, and cling to it more than I did to my own? Why would you turn water to wine, Jesus?

In the café, he sits. He stares. But I am still in Europe. In Asia. The images of countries I never visited stream past my eyes.

—

While in Thailand, I had very little money. Those four lanky creature-girls who lounged on the beach like sirens, and whose beautiful white arms and names, amid the anonymity of everyone, surfaced, slowly, like individual badges by which I could tell them apart, they told me I was wise. I told them they were beautiful and light and airy. I watched them in the morning, walk from their tiny, rented bungalow to worship a sun-god, positioning their bodies into perfect statues. One position was called Child's Pose, where they prostrated, and their arms like wings lifted, then fell snugly to their sides. I was reminded of my father. Once, I had seen him prostrate, pray to Allah, but religion was a barred phenomenon in my household— though my mother wore Allah on a gold necklace around her neck and though my eldest sister, in high school, picked up the expressions *Allaaaaaah* and *Say Walahi*—and so with my father, I never spoke of religion. But I watched these girls, and it was no different, how they moved their bodies for meaning. I'd looked down then at my cup of instant coffee and seen my arm covered in ugly, long, black hairs, made wispy now from so many years of waxing, but still there.

"They don't turn paler in the sun? I thought everyone's hair turned paler in the sun," one of them had said, with thin, turned-down lips and judgment that was only accidental.

In the afternoon, we watched the waves and talked about tsunamis.

"The end of the world is coming. That's what I think," one of them said.

"I think." My voice had aged. It sounded broken to me. Their four young bodies around our little wooden patio table leaned in closer to me, and I tried so hard not to envy them, or hate them because they were nice, they were so nice to me.

"What?"

"Yeah, what?"

"This obsession with the end of the world. It's not the end end. Sometimes I think we're so afraid of the Earth continuing on without us that we have to believe we'll see it all go down with us." It was a thought I had never thought until that moment, with the sun above us and our waiter, small and tan with big teeth, delivering our stir-fried noodles and chopsticks.

"You know, I always thought maybe that's why insects scare us so much yet we're, like, so big. Like, they always survive. No matter what. And we won't." The quiet one with dark eyes spoke. She ashed her cigarette into the ashtray between us with one leg folded against her chest.

"They're more evolved than us, for sure."

"Right. I guess. In a way."

"They know how to survive."

A gust of wind blew through us, tipping their empty plastic water glasses. Mine was filled with water, still, and stayed put.

"Survival of the fittest," another one of them said.

I watched the cups fly off the table and be pushed farther out onto the beach, where a group of young men walked in flip-flops and bathing suits, laughing at the sudden surge of sand that had got into their eyes and mouths. The girls watched them walk, and the boys noticed them too. They smiled at each other, and it calmed me. The guys walked up the steps into the restaurant to speak with us. And I, the only dark head among the fair, knew my role as the exotic one to taste.

—

I followed the Yogis a while longer. "For fun," I followed them along the narrow streets where the Thai prostitutes sit and blink and hope for johns they don't want to fuck, and I thought, I am not like them, and again, and again, nearly every feverish night, they led me dancing with them. Again, the girls, sirens with long hair, their transformation by then for me was complete and they danced on borrowed legs, they belonged someplace deep down below the water, where they could breathe.

But it was comfortable and familiar to be surrounded by women instead of men.

"I was raped once," one of them revealed to me one night. I told her I was so sorry. "I'm not," she said. She smiled, so brightly, and let her hair hang loose. "We all were. That's how I got into Yoga. That's how I met all these girls. A support group, sort of."

But then the shadow of the man came to us one night. We slept on hammocks inside of mosquito nets in a makeshift cabin on the beach in a different town. The girls had gotten drunk on the beach with another group of tourists, waving their oh-my-Gods like boobs at Mardi Gras.

"Teach us how you do it. I feel like everyone here wants to fuck you," they'd begged me, sipping on warm beer, giggling and bubbling the way nice girls are taught to.

"Just don't give a fuck. Just." And when people start to view you as wise, you start to believe you are. "Just feel the weight of you until that becomes your power."

Then in the ocean-loud, pulsing heat of 2 a.m., the shadow was slipping into one of their beds—the one whose body she claimed had been filled with water at birth instead of bone, the one who had reminded me of my sister that first night these raped women had saved me from a maybe-rape, and she was laughing. "What are you doing? How did you find me here?" She laughed again.

"Shhhh," he said. "Shhh."

I listened to them. She was quiet. He was entirely silent and I wanted to tell her never, ever trust a man who makes no sounds in bed. And I wanted to know if she was okay. But I was afraid. I think back to that night when maybe I could have been made a hero—I felt that I should have stopped it. She never fought him. I never heard a no. I never heard a condom wrapper tearing. I heard only the bones of a knee crack, the sandy floorboard as he lifted his body into the cot—the darkness that was absolute. And the breathing I heard was my own. And I thought of the sister I was never kind to. I was never kind to her, as a little girl, or teenager. And I didn't know, had she died a virgin? Had she ever done a thing she didn't want to do? And I hadn't known her favourite colour when she died. She was so decisive and yet so changeable. Did she regret it, her last favourite, in her last second?

"Hello?"

The voice was not hers. She was lost, in some other, ethereal land, dark yet orange, she was blind.

It was him. The voice of my shadow-man. I tumbled out of bed and ran, I ran foot against floorboard to the wet, cool sand. Water rushed over my legs, and groups of tourists still partied farther off on in the distance. And is there any place so infinite as a dark black sky over dark black water? I saw fire in the distance, where the people danced a dance that was an omen and a sadness. My nightgown, wet, billowed around me. I was waist-deep now. I shot my neck backwards and looked straight up at all the stars, and it was the closest to outer space I'll ever feel, the closest to God I ever got, the loneliest, the most insignificant I have ever felt. And I wondered if this is what she wished to touch on too early, too curious for her own good, my sister.

"Are you okay?" The man shouted from the edge of the beach. And to find solace in a man, I thought, like my mother, my older sister, my friends, is the worst cowardice of all.

"Kora! Did you have a nightmare! Come back!" one of the girls called out. She was made shadow next to him.

I started to laugh.

"You're supposed to sing me into the ocean, not out of it, mermaids," I shouted. I was laughing or crying. But the waves carried the words away into dark. I swam sideways, hair matted against my head, toward the party that, when I reached it, was just smoke and a few voices speaking intensely in French. They stared up at me the way raccoons do at dawn.

I imagined making love to the shadow-man, him folding me like a sheet of clean, white paper, having a baby. I wanted to call A--- and ask her why I kept fantasizing for things I did not want.

"Because you do want them," she'd have said.

But she's wrong.

In the morning, the one whose mouth slanted downwards talked about how much bigger her boobs had gotten since she was in high school. Another complained of a sunburn. All of them begged me to come.

"You can be a Master, too," they sang.

—

What I never would have revealed to them was how much I did not want them to leave me. The following morning, the sky was the colour of jaundiced skin, and one after the other, their warm lips kissed my tired cheek while we watched the Pacific Ocean crash against our dirty feet.

"Did you know," the darkest-eyed one said, "that apparently in the *Odyssey* by Homer, that whole time that Odysseus travels the seven seas, or whatever, there's no mention of blue. It's always grey."

"Yeah. Blue wasn't invented yet."

"Are you stupid?" They laughed like bits of light falling from the sky. "Not invented! That doesn't make any sense. You mean, we hadn't, like, developed the idea of it yet so then we couldn't perceive it."

"Same thing. That's what I meant."

A long pause and a momentary sliver of sun escaped behind a cloud.

"Do you think the world looked like it does today every day then, to them? I mean, like, how much power do words really give a thing?"

They turned to me for wisdom but I was only twenty-nine. Their bodies crowded me.

"I don't know," I said. I wouldn't cry.

"We'll miss you," they whispered. The one who looked and breathed like Kimia slipped a paper into my jeans pocket. Another said, "I did it last night. I did it and it was magical."

How close to the edge is the magic of life? But the time for wisdom was finished. Instead, to each of them, like a slow, unsteady cat stretching awake, I said, "Be careful," and thought of my mother.

"Byeeeeeeee," their voices pierced the humid air between us as they packed into a cab and left for the airport.

I phoned my parents. This was the first time since England I had spoken to them. My mother cried. My mother called me flower in a language I hadn't heard spoken since March. Then my father came on.

"Are you happy?" he asked. I remember so distinctly because I couldn't remember him ever asking me before.

"Since when do you care?" He said nothing. I tried again. I said, "I mean."

"You think this is cool? What you're doing? I know what you're doing," he said.

"What am I doing?"

He did that Iranian thing with his mouth to express shock and disappointment . . . something about the tongue against the roof of the mouth. So much shame in one sound. I felt small and full of rage.

"What am I doing? Tell me. What am I doing?"

You know.

You know, you know.

PHILIP HUYNH

THE FORBIDDEN PURPLE CITY

I do not have any appetite for the sentimental music of a bygone era, and so I was leery of picking up the two musicians from the airport. Their youth ran counter to their reputedly stoic commitment to *vong co*, that form of tonal melancholy developed by a Mekong Delta composer almost a hundred years ago. The idea of these dove-cheeked throwbacks frankly smacked of disingenuousness, exploiting our audience's emotional blind spots with old formulas. And though it was Tiet Linh who had originally booked this husband-and-wife duo for our New Year's concert here in Vancouver, Tiet Linh was in no state to tend to the details of transportation. She left that to me.

In addition to their luggage, the man carried two hard, black instrument cases; one for him, I thought, and one for her. The couple looked like slick moderns, in their late twenties or early thirties, bleary-eyed from their flight, but well dressed and coiffed. Both were overcompensating with wool jackets, knitted caps, scarves, and leather gloves. In fact it rarely ever snows in Vancouver, though when I led the couple outside into the drizzle they both hugged themselves as if they had under-dressed. I admit I was touched by this gesture, perhaps more so than I ever could be by their music. I have lived in Vancouver for over thirty years now, and had forgotten just how cold those first winters were for me. I hurried them into my taxicab, the meter turned off because this was a personal errand.

In my cab we discussed our common connection with Tiet Linh. I didn't ask them about what life is like back in the old country, not even the customary questions about the weather, for though I have not returned in over thirty years, I have gained a sufficient sense of contemporary Vietnam through the Internet. Perhaps they took my silence on that matter as an aversion to conversation in general, because for the rest of the ride they kept their chatter to themselves.

"I hope they'll be okay. The air here is very dry," said the man (though, as I had said, it was drizzling).

"You worry about them, and not my throat?" said the woman.

"You can take care of your own throat; they can't."

"You shouldn't have brought her. You never listen."

"She's safer with me, even here."

"I wish I felt the same way."

"Don't talk silly."

None of this talk made sense to me at the time, but later I found out that the man was speaking about his *danh bau*, the single-stringed instrument that he kept in one of the cases. The other instrument was an electric moon lute. I know something of the danh bau: that when played by a master, the monochrome has the resonance of a woman's vocal cords.

"I will not sing if you play her."

"Don't worry," he said. "She'll stay in the case."

The woman seemed to be comforted by his words, but the peace only lasted for a moment before they started arguing about some point of music theory that I could not grasp. She complained about how he always tries to lose her by playing in *day kep*, the key of the man. He made some fresh retort, and I heard a scratching of plastic that made me worried she was going to fling open the door, but then he said something else that seemed to soothe her.

Perhaps it was disrespectful for them to speak so openly about themselves in the company of an old man, but I didn't mind their self-absorption. Such was their licence as artists, and, yes, I also took comfort in listening to the ebbs and flows of a young couple's intimate dispute, as one sometimes does in a sad memory.

I dropped them off at Tiet Linh's house. The lights of her East Vancouver duplex were off. I was so relieved when her daughter answered the door, but began to worry again when she said that Tiet Linh had retired early. Tiet Linh had become increasingly removed from our affairs ever since Anh Binh, her husband, passed away six months ago.

"Would you like me to leave her a message?" said the daughter.

"Yes, that her guests are here."

"Guests?"

"The musicians that your mother arranged for. All the way from Vietnam. They are staying here, no?"

"Oh, dear," said the daughter, thinking with Anh Binh's darting eyebrows—so much her father's daughter. "Bac Gia, leave the two with me."

I miss Anh Binh dearly for all he has done for me over the years, but despite my mourning I am still living up to my responsibilities to ensure the success of the New Year's celebrations. Am I selfish for wishing that Tiet Linh would do the same?

Tiet Linh and I work together as concert promoters, though each of us would deny being "partners" in any sense of that word. We do not share the profits from our mutual labours (there aren't any), though Tiet Linh often jokes that we share the liabilities of each other's company. That does not a partnership make, I say.

We've had our disagreements over the years as to the musicians we wanted to promote, and not only because of our own aesthetic preferences, but because such choices would bear on the composition of our audience—the very community we sought to create on these errant weekend nights. In the late 1980s we filled the stage of a neighbourhood house on Victoria Drive with old-fashioned *Cai Luong* singers— they were in easy supply as I recall, all those keening lungs in high-necked silk *ao dai* dresses—and were thusly rewarded with a lukewarm assemblage of the curious, idle elderly. In the early 1990s I took the initiative of promoting New Wave acts, and we were able to fill the gyms of various East Vancouver elementary schools with Vietnamese covers of Krisma. Tiet Linh, however, thought we had gone too far with attracting a certain segment of the floppy-haired youth with their glow sticks and marijuana cigarillos, driving everyone else out into the moonlight. After much tussling back and forth between us, we have settled on a variety-show format (perhaps redolent of the *Paris by Night* series) featuring a rotating dish of singers, but always with The Aquamarines as the backup band. This has worked well: You can now find all the generations at one of our concerts.

Whenever Anh Binh saw us arguing, he would smile with the masked equanimity of a dentist (he was, in fact, a dentist) and shake his head. Arguments over whether, for instance, the reds and yellows of the old South Vietnamese flag should always appear somewhere on the grandstand. Or whether, as master of ceremonies, I should stop wearing the same brown suit and bespoke tie (I believed my trademark attire was important for brand recognition, while Tiet Linh thought it begged more the mood of Sunday church). Although Anh Binh often played the mediator, to him our fights were at once absurdly quotidian and impracticably philosophical.

I knew that Anh Binh was dying when Tiet Linh and I stopped arguing—when she started nodding at whatever I said, looking for ghosts.

We were all young together in Hue, the old imperial capital in central Vietnam. During the war, in that awful year of 1968, when Hue was held captive by the Communists for a month (how awful we thought that month was, but how little did we know what was ahead), I was living with my wife in my family's home, and Tiet Linh was living with Anh Binh in his. We were all in the same neighbourhood just south of the Perfume River, near the university, where Tiet Linh and I studied literature and art history, respectively, and Anh Binh was studying to be a dentist.

My wife, meanwhile, was already making a living as a nurse

and bone-setter (a trade passed on by her father to his only child). My wife's name is Ngoc, meaning jewel, and her mind was as sharp as one; she was a practical jewel: a diamond, not an emerald—not only beautiful, but able to drill.

The Communists came during Tet, the Vietnamese New Year. The noise that in my memories could be heard above the firecrackers was the teeth of the old women chatter-chiming from door to door of our neighbourhood, like electricity running down a live wire, for it was the old women who felt the advance of the Viet Cong deep inside them—all those angry sons coming home to roost upon their mothers' ringing bones. The Communists were looking for people like Tiet Linh and me, the intellectuals and the Catholics. We escaped through the back while the cadres knocked on our front doors.

We scrambled on foot down dusty roads flooded with a humanity that was equal parts panic and resignation, as the Communists took over the Citadel north of the Perfume River, and then the south bank. The Communists had planted their flag high behind the stone walls of the Ngo Mon gate, and we always made sure our backs were to it. We made it out of the city to a farmhouse in Anh Binh's ancestral village, all four of us crowding in with Anh Binh's aunts, uncles, grandparents, and assorted nephews and cousins.

During the month that it took the Americans and the South Vietnamese to retake Hue, both Anh Binh and Ngoc worked in the village hospital, where they tended to the overflowing civilian casualties. Anh Binh even conducted rudimentary surgeries. A doctor was a doctor, even if he was a dentist. It was no time to make fine discernments.

Meanwhile Tiet Linh and I hid on the farm. During our first days we helped with the rice planting, though neither of us were trained to work on our haunches in the flooded paddies, and we both took turns falling head-first in the mud, imprinting our bodies with the crushed stalks of newly transplanted seedlings. Mostly we read while waiting like children for our spouses to return from work. While we argued the finer points of Sartre or whether the French treated the Vietnamese worse than the Vietnamese treated their Cham minority, our spouses cut into bone or swept away entrails. They always came home late and too tired to talk, often with traces of blood on their clothes to mark their day. How could two such soft-spoken and practical people be married to the likes of Tiet Linh and me? Anh Binh would retire with his wife in the main house, while Ngoc and I slept on the packed-dirt floor of the kitchen, where Ngoc would stare at the thatched roof in darkened amazement. She was a city girl and wondered where the chimney was for the stove that we rested our feet against, with its feel of cool metal.

"It's a thatched roof," I said. "The smoke rises right through it." Even after what she must have seen each day at the hospital, Ngoc still had the energy to look at me with her wide eyes of disbelief, but she did not argue. This discussion of porousness made me think of the Communist invasion, and I talked of how the Communists weren't bringing us a revolution but, like the French, were just trying to "civilize" us in their own terrifying ways. Ngoc replied with a purr of breath. She had left me for her dreamland, and soon I fell asleep as well. Amazing how still those nights were, with that many people under one roof, the only noise the soft burps of distant shelling.

When we returned to Hue after the month-long siege, my home remained one of the few in the neighbourhood that was still standing. Outside, bicycles wobbled over tank tracks. Before entering, we paid our respects to the Spirit of the Soil as if we were building a completely new home. Everything inside the house was destroyed. Books and photos were ripped down the middle, as though by a petulant child. The wires of anything electronic were torn out of their guts. By this, the Communists were saying what they would have done if they could have laid their hands on us. I followed Ngoc into our bedroom like we were newlyweds—carefully following the tradition of not letting the bride step on the groom's shadow. It was only much later that we realized the extent of the civilian massacre during the occupation, that the hastily turned soil of some of the bare fields in Hue hid mass graves.

We were only days away from the New Year's concert and I was left to do everything. Tiet Linh and I used to have a clear division of labour: I was in charge of the venue, and she would take care of the musicians. I booked the high-school gym or the community hall, rented the sound and strobe machines, called up Ba Chau for the *banh mi* sandwich catering, made sure enough glossy New Year's tickets were printed. Tiet Linh made sure that the musicians were happy. I preferred my job.

Now that they could not reach Tiet Linh, the artists started calling my cellphone at all hours of the day. One diva called me while I was on shift in my cab, demanding to know why she was in the lineup right after another diva who sings in the same tea-gargling style. How should I know? Then there is Ong Cho, the civil-engineer-cum-balladeer, who called me while I was at peace with my bowl of *bun bo Hue* to remind me to bring some marbles, with which he plugs his ears so that he could better concentrate on stage. Why doesn't he just supply his own marbles? I tried to keep my composure, but the last straw was when Johnny Nguyen called, our sole remaining homage to the New Wave that we have on retainer, though he has gone bald and continually defies our ban on Styrofoam cups.

"What do you want?" I said.

"Just saying *chao*, Bac Gia. How's it going?"

"How would I know? I'm on the stool."

"That's cool."

Tiet Linh *oi*, wherever you are, you must come out of your hiding.

All that Hue is for me now is the Forbidden Purple City, that centre within the nested squares of fortresses of the Citadel. It's all that my memory holds. For instance, I've been having the hardest time remembering the tamarind tree that grew outside my home, the only one miraculously still standing on my block after the siege. I've tried to locate my neighbourhood on Google Street View, but it has completely changed, and what I saw in its place was shiny, bustling. Most of the videos on YouTube about Hue are of the Citadel and all the nostalgia that it provokes. Or rather sentimentality, for I recently learned that the word *nostalgia* pertains to memory, and most people who use YouTube as a resource have no real memories related to the Citadel. If forgetting about the Forbidden Purple City would mean that my other memories of Hue would be uncovered, then I would choose forgetting about the Forbidden Purple City.

But then again, perhaps I am also guilty of "sentimentality," because the palaces of the Forbidden Purple City had long burned down by my time, even before the siege of Hue. I had seen it only as bare ground marked by loose foundations.

It was once the Emperor's inner sanctum, and during the siege the Communists used it as an operations base. Most of the surrounding palaces were also levelled by the siege's end. This was the state of the Citadel as I remember it best: the crushed bricks within the piles of timber, the scent of ancient ironwood columns split down their seams, releasing an oddly fresh smell of pine. This was the smell of my livelihood.

I managed to escape being drafted by the South Vietnamese Army, and a couple of years after the siege I was employed by the provincial Restoration Committee. I spent most of my days, nights even, within the Citadel's stone walls. By this time the floating bodies had been pulled out of the moats, and peasants were cultivating a water-borne spinach in the Royal Canal. I camped on these grounds as part of my work, though *restoration* may not be the right word. The war was still on and resources were scarce. *Preservation* is perhaps a more suitable term, as it was not so much a matter of rebuilding, as trying to clear the rubble into coherent piles throughout the palace grounds, *vo* bricks and tiles on one side, timber on another—mindful that some of the peasant volunteers were just there to run off with ironwood to warm their hearths. I carried a French service pistol to wave at marauders and slowly built a team of men I trusted. Anh Binh was one of them. He volunteered on weekends to erect scaffolding to hold up the imperial roofs, and kept the young men in line. He was paler than most of the labourers, having spent most of his days indoors, but he had a solid build and a greater stamina for hardship.

We did what we could. Under my watch the old palaces did not rise again, but neither did any of them fall. Everything changed once again in 1975, when the Communists took over for good. At first they wanted to destroy all the remaining palaces as symbols of imperialism, but Ho Chi Minh himself saved the Citadel, saying that because it was built on the backs of peasants it belonged to the peasants. As a restorer I was suddenly doing the People's work. My life was preserved. I had hope.

I worked for the Communists until I fled the country in 1980. This was before UNESCO became involved, with their Western standards of original materials and ancient means; instead the Communists favoured jerry-rigged methods with whatever was available. By this time most of the original ironwood columns had been reaped by the marauders (I was helpless to stop them—they knew I wouldn't shoot), and the Communists were now replacing most of the wooden beams with a type of ferro-concrete and painting over whatever original gilt was left with an industrial paint from China.

Ngoc was always worried I would shoot my mouth off at a cadre with a bourgeois remark and be hauled off to the re-education camps. The way the Communists were handling the project did make me feel like I was standing on uncertain ground, and this feeling manifested itself one morning in 1977, when, during a rooftop foot patrol, I tripped over a piece of jutting concrete. I broke my ankle. Ngoc, so busy at work, now had to set my bones for free while I lay on our bed biting on a rolled-up reed mat. She rubbed a paste made from her father's secret recipe over my heel and up my shin that dried into a cast, then secured my mess of a foot with bamboo splints and bandages. I had made it through the whole war without breaking a bone in my body. Now I stayed in bed for several weeks—the worst time in my life. For my wife it was the best time, she said, because for once she knew exactly where I was.

Once my ankle healed and I was able to hobble on my own power, I returned to the Citadel. My absence had done nothing to stop the onward rush of restoration by the Communists. I still slept on the grounds of the Forbidden Purple City, but now it was once a fortnight and largely for nostalgic reasons, with the marauders more or less gone. The palaces were more beautiful at night, when their perfect forms were backlit by the moon and one didn't notice the broken roof tiles of the Emperor's Writing Pavilion or the bamboo scaffolding holding up the roof of the Palace of Supreme Harmony. At night the workmen's laundry hanging from the moon-shaped windows turned into horse-dragons.

One night I was standing in a minor pavilion overlooking a lotus pond and contemplating its eerie stillness when, through the beating horn-song of the cicadas, I heard the approach of footsteps. I was hobbling on a cane, did not have my service pistol, and thought my ghost had come for me. And then I heard a familiar sniffling.

"What are you doing here?" I said.

It was Tiet Linh. She was carrying a lantern, royal yellow and diamond-shaped. The size of a pineapple. She held it out toward me—a gift.

"I'm worried about you," she said. "Hobbling about in the dark. You're going to break your one good foot."

I didn't believe this was why she came, of course, but I received her gift all the same. I put my lighter to the wick inside the lantern, and hung it off the lip of a carp-shaped rain sluice on the roof. I had not realized how dark the night was until that moment. Now I could see the flicker of the dragonflies just above the lily pads. "You didn't come here just to give me a lamp, did you?"

"I came to see the restoration."

Again, I didn't believe her; why would she come at night? "Why are you interested?"

"History students don't have a monopoly over history," she said, referring to our ongoing quibble over which of our respective subjects was the superior undertaking.

"The Communists are building an approximation," I said. "Which is the same as a desecration." We looked out into the darkness toward the flag tower. The cicadas were getting louder, as if closing in.

"It's a desecration now," she said.

"No, it is in ruins now," I said. "That is something completely different." All the destruction around us was a result of war, which in Vietnam was a natural occurrence. What the Communists wanted to do was unnatural. To reclaim the past they were willing to sweep away reality.

"Are they going to rebuild the Forbidden Purple City?"

"*Goi oi*, don't get me started," I said.

We went into the altar space of the pavilion and looked out into the flat grounds that were once the Forbidden Purple City. Rice paddies took up a good part of the grounds now.

She was smiling wickedly at me. "Imagine what it must have looked like," she said.

"I can't even begin," I said. There were no blueprints left of it, no photos. I feared that the Communists were just going to make something up from thin air. Probably just a copycat of the Beijing palaces.

"You can begin with this," said Tiet Linh. She pulled something out of her handbag: another gift, this time with a royal yellow fringe. It was a *National Geographic*. "I found this in my grandfather's bedroom," she said. "It's from the 1930s." She opened the pages, which crackled as if new. "Here, look. They took pictures of the Forbidden Purple City before it burned down."

I held the magazine and took my time turning the pages for each photo, then looked back out to the rice paddies. I could see it all clearly now. The court of honour where the stone mandarins and horses were aligned, the covered walkways where the eunuchs tiptoed toward their conspiracies. The imperial chamber with its posh linens over smooth, hard beds. Even now I see these rooms in my dreams and wake up holding my stomach.

Then, as quickly as her spirits lifted, Tiet Linh's face cracked. "Anh Binh is leaving me," she said. She was tearing.

"Don't be silly."

"I don't trust him anymore," she said.

(At the time I had no context for her statement, but the next year, in 1978, Anh Binh disappeared. Tiet Linh kept mum about his whereabouts, even let us believe he was dead, until we found out that he had re-emerged on the other side of the ocean, in Vancouver. He had escaped by boat under cover of night.)

"You must have had a fight, that's all," I said. "You should go home. I'm sure Anh Binh is worried about you."

"He can wait," she said. She wanted me to show her the grounds as I knew them.

I took her to a little pontoon boat hidden in the corner of the lotus pond, and I pretended to be the Emperor and she one of my eunuchs. I paddled, we serenaded the moon, and Tiet Linh recited her favourite lines from *The Tale of Kieu*:

> *Due to my dismal generosity in past lives,*
> *I have to accept much suffering as compensation in this life.*
> *My body has been violated as a broken pot,*
> *I have to sell my body to repay for my mournful fate.*

"How depressing," I said, though she sang the lines lightly, like a summer lullaby.

"Do you remember during the siege, when your wife and my husband would come home together, always tired and silent?"

"It was another life," I said.

"Didn't you ever wonder about them?"

"Not at all," I said. "Never." And I meant it.

I love the English word *hope*. My English sentence-making is very good, though to this day my passengers sometimes have trouble understanding me because of my thick accent. I love the English language though, how irreducible it is. *Hope* is true English, unlike *optimism*, which is an immigrant from the Latin world, with its messy roots in sight and whatnot and its mutt pedigree with other terms, like *optics*, *option*, etc. Such a pure word is *hope* that it cannot be broken down any further and stands for only itself—like those primal words meant to invoke animal sounds. *Meow. Ruff. Hope.* Even the

Vietnamese term for "hope," *hy vong*, isn't so pure. Taken alone, *hy* can mean "rare," and *vong* can mean anything from an "echo" to an "absurdity."

A rare echo. A rare absurdity. That is "hope" in Vietnamese.

There was a knock on my door the night before the New Year's Day concert. I grabbed a Club before answering. I keep a few extra Clubs around for they are handy beyond securing the steering wheel of my cab. I rent a laneway house in East Vancouver with tin-thin walls and about two cab-lengths long, with my bedroom window hugging the property line by the back alleyway. One can never be too cautious.

It was the musician—the man—hugging one of his instrument cases, the one in the shape of a small coffin. The danh bau. The overhead lamp illuminated scratches on his face, a wicked play of shadows deepening the grooves, darkening his tears into blood drops.

"Bac Gia," he said, "I apologize for the disruption. But I was given your address, and I—"

"Your wife did this?" I knew the answer, but took some satisfaction when he nodded to confirm my insights into the artistic temperament.

"May we stay the night?" he said. I let him in, though there was no room for both of us to sleep unless I moved my kitchen table outside, which I was loath to do. I surrendered my bed to him, and after he took his shoes off he quickly fell asleep, his instrument by his side as if he had always lived here. I tried to sleep in my cab but soon gave up and turned on the ignition.

I drove to Tiet Linh's house. I parked in the back alley and jimmied the gate to the yard. I knew that it would be futile if

I rung any of the doorbells—her daughter would surely answer the door and shoo me away—and so I reached down to the ground and gathered some pebbles. I took the back-porch stairs up to the second-floor landing, stopping at the sight of black metal gleaming between the wooden steps. It was a new Broil King, completely untarnished by charcoal dust or oil splatters. Anh Binh must have bought it just before he died.

At the top of the landing I tossed the pebbles one at a time at Tiet Linh's bedroom window (like the way I throw bread at the swans in Vancouver's Lost Lagoon). Her ghostly pallor was undeniable as she drew back the blinds. In the moonlight haze she looked just as she did that night in the Forbidden Purple City.

"I didn't come here to serenade you," I said. "And I'm not here to offer you any pity."

"That's fine, as long as you're not looking for any from me."

"You can't just disappear."

"If it's about the musician, he has nowhere to go. You can send him to a hotel and bill me."

"I knew it was a bad idea to get these young people pretending to be old-time musicians," I said. "It's unnatural." I could tell that what I said enlivened her, because her cheeks darkened into what in the daylight would have been a bright vermillion.

"Unnatural! You always claimed to be a historian, but you never had an appreciation for the old crafts. You have no ear for it."

"Oh! Oh!" I said. "Don't get me started!" But by now we couldn't stop from entering that dark debate about whether vong co music had any value. I argued more vehemently against the music than I actually felt. Tiet Linh's daughter came to the window, only to be waved away by Tiet Linh, who was in mid-volley about some esoteric point. We were waking up the dogs in the neighbourhood, but we didn't care. It was quite some time before I walked back down the stairs to my cab, and I took one last look at the Broil King.

"You can't just disappear!" I said again, but by now Tiet Linh's window was closed and all the lights were out.

Among the four of us, Tiet Linh and I were known as the dreamers and Anh Binh and Ngoc were known as the schemers. Anh Binh was the first one to escape Vietnam, and Tiet Linh followed him the next year. Anh Binh then came up with a plan to sponsor me to Canada as his brother, even though we were unrelated. We shared the same last name—Nguyen—and it didn't matter that about half of Vietnam shared this surname because his scheme worked. I would just have to find a way to get to Vancouver.

When I told Ngoc to pack her things, she told me to go ahead without her. I was furious with her. She said she had a few things to tend to first with family and work, but that I shouldn't delay in going and that she would join me soon thereafter. I left by boat with an uneasy feeling in my stomach—one that didn't go away during the five months I spent at a refugee camp in Hong Kong, nor when I finally arrived in Vancouver. I had forgotten to bring a picture of Ngoc, not even a little wallet-sized photo. I thought it a funny occurrence then. No matter, I thought, I would see her soon enough.

Ngoc passed away a year after I arrived in Vancouver. She was in fact ill before then, and knew of her fate back in Vietnam when I asked her to leave with me. Just like Anh Binh, she was a practical schemer, and she wanted to leave me with my dreams unscathed.

I still dream, of course, of the Forbidden Purple City. These days the Citadel is being restored with the expertise and funding of UNESCO and of countries as far flung as Korea, Germany, and Poland. Now they use vo bricks and traditional tiles in the reconstruction. Ironwood has returned to replace the ferro-concrete, buffalo glue is now used, and the palaces are mortared now by an authentic mixture of sugar cane molasses, lime, and local sand. I've been watching the progress on YouTube, how the Forbidden Purple City is rising in its vivid red splendour amongst a background of original palaces standing in dull relief. For a small price, tourists can dress like the Emperor and take photos in the palaces with a consort of actors playing eunuchs. With all the chaotic occurrences on YouTube, I can't tell sometimes what is a documentary of the reconstruction, and what is an historical melodrama. But all together it is like the war never happened. It is like there was never any reason for us to leave the country.

When I arrived home from Tiet Linh's house the danh bau player was gone. My first thought was to call the police, but he had taken nothing from me. Then I worried about his own safety, but there was nothing I could do. Tiet Linh would not answer my texts, nor my phone messages.

The next evening I walked to the site of the New Year's concert, a high-school gymnasium not too far from where I live. As is my routine, I arrived a couple of hours before the start. I carried an uneasy feeling in my belly at the chaos that would reign in Tiet Linh's absence. To my great relief, though, the ticket-punch girl was already there, resplendent in her ao dai and setting up her table at the entrance. Inside the gym, Ba Chau rolled in her banh mi sandwiches on trays and my trusted volunteers were tying colourful streamers. Someone had already placed a small *Hoa Mai* tree on the stage and hung red ribbons off its yellow-blossomed branches. Men from the light and strobe company were moving cables across the polished gym floor and put before me a clipboard with a voucher to sign. I should have known, of course, that the world would go on without the likes of Tiet Linh and me.

Soon The Aquamarines arrived, our long-standing backup band consisting of former South Vietnamese soldiers in hep-cat berets and fedoras, unpacking their drumkits and guitars. Then I heard a commotion in the back dressing room and braced my stomach again. The divas had already arrived. As I walked to their rooms, their voices echoed off the plastered brick wall of the hallway. The Cai Luong singers, the engineer-cum-balladeer, the aging New Waver: their voices were all bouncing off the walls.

And one more, one very welcome voice: Tiet Linh was among them. "We were wondering about you," she said. They were all laughing and Tiet Linh's eyes were puffy with dried tears. They had been talking about Anh Binh. By now Tiet Linh had already arbitrated the lineup and had taken care of all the musicians' pastoral needs: marbles for the engineer, Styrofoam cups for the New Waver.

But there was one thing. "Where are the vong co musicians?" I asked. For this Tiet Linh had no answer. "He came back to my house last night," said Tiet Linh, "and then the two left together. Who knows if they'll show up?"

"The artistic temperament knows no boundaries," I said.

"At least of decorum," she said.

I left Tiet Linh to her musicians and tended to the details of the stage. There were too many problems to deal with in the time remaining, but when the rafter lights were lowered and the strobe lights came on, I could no longer see any imperfection. The crowd filtered in and took their seats at the long cafeteria tables, and I took my customary seat off to the side. All the generations came, from grandparents my age in suits and ties or ao dais and evening pearls, to young people who wore as much mascara and glitter on their clothes as the performers did. The old danced the cha-cha to the standards, while the young sang along to new numbers.

The evening flowed as harmoniously as any other until midway through the concert the rafter lights came back on. Most of The Aquamarines then left the stage, except for the guitarist, who replaced his instrument with a moon lute. The rafter lights dimmed again and the spotlight froze on a resplendent couple in ancient dress. Our two vong co players had come after all.

The man stood behind his danh bau, its single string untouched yet already resounding, its buffalo-horn spout rising from its gourd, its lacquered soundboard shimmering in the strobe light. The woman turned to her husband and appeared to smile before taking to the microphone. Tiet Linh joined me at the table, looking eternal in her own ao dai. The crowd cheered as soon as the first notes of "*Da Co Hoai Lang*" were released from the moon lute. This was the original song that started off the whole genre, written by Cao Van Lau, who was forced by his mother to dispense with his wife after three years of a barren marriage. A legend persists that the poor composer would choke up every day he brought home his catch of crustaceans, because his wife was no longer present to sort the shrimps from the crabs. Old men wiped away tears when the singer chimed in above the moon lute. For much of the song her husband stood still and considered his danh bau with a silent stroke of his finger against the spout. When finally he struck his first chord against the single string, his wife did not crack or hurl herself off the stage as I expected. Rather, she sang alongside the danh bau, whose chord stood up as its own voice against hers, in a true duet of mourning.

The lights stayed low when the song was finished, and a small girl came up to give pink flowers to both the wife and the husband. I looked over at Tiet Linh and her lips were crisply sealed with a look of endurance. How far we have made it, she seemed to say. I thought about how I had not had a chance to properly comfort her in the months since her husband and my good friend had passed away. I wanted to tell her that she didn't have to be alone. I wanted to say what I would have wanted to hear when my own wife passed away. I opened my mouth, but no words came, just a trembling of my lips.

"You don't have to say anything," said Tiet Linh.

I knew this was an act of kindness on her part.

I thought of our lives together, both on this and the other shore. I looked down at the table. "I can't see Ngoc's face any-more," I said. "I've tried everything I can, but I can't find her in my memory. It's been so long now."

Tiet Linh held my hand to still it. Then she touched my chin and tilted it up toward the stage as the next singer took the microphone, as the drummer lifted his drumsticks.

JESS TAYLOR

TWO SEX ADDICTS FALL IN LOVE

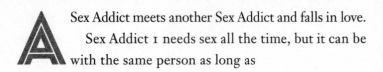Sex Addict meets another Sex Addict and falls in love. Sex Addict 1 needs sex all the time, but it can be with the same person as long as

1. It's interesting
2. The person smells good
3. They both come at least once almost every time
4. It is done in many new ways and with a sense of adventure

Sex Addict 1 knows she loves Sex Addict 2 forever.
Sex Addict 2 needs sex all the time, but hopefully

1. With as many people as possible
2. In as many different ways as possible
3. In unexpected circumstances
4. Without needing to worry about anyone's feelings

Sex Addict 2 cares about Sex Addict 1's feelings and is constantly thinking about the lists. Sex Addict 2 also isn't sure he believes in love—he's never seen it at least, despite feeling the way he does with Sex Addict 1. Also, how can love exist when the lists also exist?

When a Sex Addict dreams of the perfect person to love them, that person is always a Sex Addict. And, of course, at first it is perfect. Sex Addict 2 finally feels that lying does not have to be part of his addiction, that he can have sex regularly with someone he cares about and still be able to nurture his urges and have someone who will try new things, explore his fantasies, and understand his needs. Sex Addict 1 feels that sexual compatibility is probably the way to true intimacy, that the fact that she finally has someone she finds attractive, interesting, good smelling, and funny to have sex with multiple times a day must mean that they are soulmates.

One night when they are out for dinner, Sex Addict 1 congratulates Sex Addict 2 on how decent he is when they disagree—that he never yells or swears at her or even seems to get too angry. Usually, when he becomes angry or upset, he'll verbalize his feelings instead of acting out. "I'm feeling angry," he'll say. "I'm hurt by what you said." Or sometimes he'll even break down his feelings further: "I'm not angry with you. I'm just annoyed. I'm frustrated." Coming from a family of yelling and cursing and emotions that never seemed to go away, Sex Addict 1 finds this trait endearing in Sex Addict 2, and it makes her love grow. Sex Addict 2 says, "Well, I don't know what we'd really have to fight about. We seem to agree on everything."

That night they get into a fight. It is the same version of a fight that they will continue to have and that previously was a "discussion" about the fate of their relationship. Each fight comes closer to the inevitable truth: they have different items on their lists. Somehow, in deciding they are perfect for each other, Sex Addict 1 and Sex Addict 2 have fallen back into their old patterns and have been lying.

In fact, if Sex Addict 1 is honest, it isn't sex that draws her in, or even the intimacy—it's feeling like her whole body is being erased. She needs to be hugged, she needs to be held, she needs to be surrounded, she needs to smell parts of another human's body. She might not even be a sex addict at all—sometimes it's easy for her to think about other things, to let ideas be what hold her, envelop her. Sometimes she dances around the kitchen and that feels almost as good. But if her connection with Sex Addict 2 finds its basis in their mutual sex addiction, then she can never renounce her identity as a sex addict or even be more specific about what it actually is.

It is unclear if we can really frame the situation Sex Addicts 1 and 2 find themselves in as being "A sex addict meets another sex addict and falls in love." This is because if Sex Addict 2 doubts the very existence of love (or at least his own ability to love actively in a way that makes everyone involved feel good), it is doubtful that he has ever allowed himself to exist in the state of "being in love" or that, if he has, he has not allowed himself to recognize this state as being in love, or allowed himself to exist within it before rushing off to pursue his addiction.

If Sex Addict 2 has never "been in love" with Sex Addict 1,

then it is doubtful that Sex Addict 1 has ever "been in love" with Sex Addict 2. Sex Addict 1 tries to figure this situation out with her friends the way she tries to figure everything out, by speaking. She tells them about the lists. She describes the different positions she and Sex Addict 2 have used. She describes her fear of being alone and her desire to be completely encased. She gives examples of Sex Addict 2's behaviour and asks for interpretation. She gets almost the same answer, with no different diction, depending on the friend: "He doesn't seem to be a very self-aware person, whereas you seem to be! I'm amazed by your awareness." Sex Addict 1 appreciates compliments during times like this, although from the details provided about Sex Addicts 1 and 2, it's easy to see that this assessment is false.

Sex Addict 1 has not selected her friends according to the trend of picking people whom you admire professionally or want to be in some capacity, who dedicate their conversational power to the discussion of their ambitions and interests and reveal very little of their inner lives.

Sex Addict 1, while admiring her friends for their talents and abilities, has chosen her friends for their compassion, creativity, and what she (as much as she can tell, being a generally poor judge of character) thinks is their good hearts. She enjoys the long hours they spend tolerating her as she talks about herself, love, and sex. But since these are fully developed people, they would also enjoy speaking about

1. Their interests
2. Outer space
3. Animals

4. The existence of ghosts
5. New scientific discoveries
6. The upcoming election
7. Pipelines
8. A new job they may get
9. A movie they just saw
10. Their families
11. The war in Syria
12. Their health
13. A plane that went missing
14. An upcoming event that they have to go to but really don't want to go to
15. Netflix

and get frustrated by the limited nature of Sex Addict 1's focus. On some level, Sex Addict 1 also acknowledges that the crumbling partnership between her and Sex Addict 2 was always fairly shallow. "It's only about attraction and pain. Why did I ever think those things are deep? They aren't about the world, they aren't about goals, dreams, secret desires, they aren't about life or death. They aren't even about the person, not really." Her friends nod along and try to change the subject. Sex Addict 1 has exhausted her lines of support.

It's hard to say what will become of Sex Addict 2. Some of their mutual friends say they see him going for walks around the city. Some say he's learning how to be on his own. Some say he thinks about love sometimes, wonders if he's wrong, thinks that maybe he can do it. He's always been surprised by the way time moves around him, and maybe it's a new season now—it's getting colder. He blows on his hands and pushes them deeper into his pockets.

The world is also changing around Sex Addict 1. Perhaps this is because she is no longer seeing everything through the lens of sex. She always thought she was a pretty decent human being except when it came to sex, and then sometimes she did things that she didn't quite mean to do. For instance, when she first met Sex Addict 2, she informed him that he was in love with her and then tried to grab his dick through his pants underneath the table, even though they were at the bar surrounded by people and he had a girlfriend. Sex Addict 1 had also been drinking, which of course didn't help any of that behaviour, but feeling sexual like that felt like being drunk anyway, somehow uninhibited, somehow operating on instinct.

Whenever Sex Addict 1 thinks about this behaviour in isolation, she thinks that this must be the behaviour of a bad person, that it's the addiction, but then when she turns it around and looks at it another way, it seems like most every person is at least a little like that.

Other times, it's as if she's separate from herself in those moments and that there is a real split in herself and that the her who needs sex is there to destroy the her who needs tenderness, the one who needs to be shielded, hugged, cared for. Sex Addict 1 has never understood why she can't occupy both these spaces at once and thinks something must be wrong with her.

In the early morning, Sex Addict 1 goes for a run. She is trying to replace a hunger for sex with taking care of herself. Sometimes when she misses Sex Addict 2, she uses a vibrator.

These sessions can last hours, and Sex Addict 1 finds that she's able to merge sex with tenderness or at least blur the lines slightly. Not that she tries to fantasize about tenderness, but she recognizes that the very act of pleasuring herself in this way is an act of tenderness, especially if it means she's not opening herself up to Sex Addict 2 again.

As she runs in the morning she feels the same thing—the borders of her physicality break up so that the heart that has always been a little too sore in her is released and beating and her brain is quiet and sun is staining the sky all over in pink and purple and orange.

IRYN TUSHABE

A SEPARATION

O n the evening before I leave for university in Canada, I sit on the terrace of my childhood home watching Kaaka, my grandmother, make lemongrass tea. She pounds cubes of sugarcane with a weathered pestle. She empties the pulp into a large pot and tops it up with rainwater from a jerry can the same olive-green as her A-shaped tunic.

I step down from my bamboo chair and stride over to her. I lift the heavy pot and set it on a charcoal stove smouldering with red-hot embers.

"Webare kahara kangye." Kaaka thanks me in singsong Rukiga, the language of our birth. She comes from a generation of Bakiga who sing to people instead of talking because words, unlike music, can get lost.

I smile and sit back down in my creaky bamboo chair to read a copy of *National Geographic* that a British photographer sent me. His photograph of a troop of gorillas in my father's wildlife sanctuary is on the cover of the magazine, and the accompanying article quotes me blaming the Ugandan government for refusing to support our conservation efforts.

"I hope I don't get in trouble for this," I say.

Kaaka laughs the sound of tumbling water. "You flatter yourself if you think the fierce leaders of our republic have time to read foreign magazines."

She chops fresh lemongrass leaves on a tree stump, sniffing the bits in her hands before tossing them into the pan. The simmering infusion is already turning the light yellow colour of honey and will taste just as sweet. As the herb steeps, a citrusy fragrance curls into the evening like an offering. Kaaka fans the steam toward her nose and inhales noisily, closing her eyes to savour the aroma.

"The tea's ready," she says a short while later, rolling out a mat woven from dried palm fronds. She sits on it, legs outstretched, hands clasped in her lap. This is how it has always been with us. Kaaka makes the tea. I serve it.

I pull the sleeves of my oversized sweater over my fingers and lift the pan off the stove. With a ladle, I fill two mugs. I give Kaaka hers and sit down next to her, blowing on my cup before sucking hot tea into my mouth. Its sweetness has an edge.

"You'll do very well in your studies overseas." There is finality in her voice. When the invitation from the University of Regina's Department of Anthropology arrived months ago, I showed her, saying I would go only if I had her blessing. "You'll acquire some new knowledge and a whole world of wisdom."

"I'll be home for Christmas," I tell her now.

"Yes, you will. Something to look forward to."

—

Three weeks later, I'm standing by my open living room window looking down at the street, watching people go about the business of living. I arrived in Regina, Saskatchewan, at the tail end of summer. The August heat has turned my apartment into a sweltering cavern. Mr. Stevenson, the silver-haired professor who met me at the airport, will be supervising my doctoral research. He also found this Munroe Place apartment for me. I can't seem to say the street name right, though. Is it Monroe as in Marilyn Monroe, the deceased American actress? Or moon-row, like a row of moons?

Two teenage girls walk by sharing a blue slushy. The one with a thick mass of coffee-coloured hair takes a sip and hands the cup over to her friend, whose short hair is tinted the bright pink of a well-fed flamingo. Sticking out blue tongues at each other, they double over in laughter. They're wearing high-waisted shorts so short that when they bend, I glimpse the lobes of their flat-flat buttocks.

Dark clouds have gathered above the high-rise across the street as though getting ready to pounce. But the sunlight pierces their serrated margins, turning them into silver beacons.

The sound of my cellphone jolts me. The call has a Ugandan country code.

"Kaaka!" I shout into the phone. My elation keeps her name in my mouth longer, making it last.

"Harriet, it's me," my father answers, his voice loud and strident. A call from Father frightens me a little. Always, I phone him. It's never the other way around. His preferred medium of communication is email—lengthy reports with headings and subheadings. The last one had an index and a couple of footnotes about his observations of infanticide amongst chimpanzees in Kibale Forest, our sanctuary's rainforest home. Did I know that contrary to previous observations of infanticide, deadly aggression in chimpanzees is not a gender-specific trait?

"Are you there, Harriet?"

I brace myself. "I'm here."

"It's about your Kaaka." Father's voice suddenly acquires an uncharacteristic softness. "She has died."

He likes directness, my father. And sharp things. He has a prized collection of spears and *pangas* in his office that he says our forefathers carried with them when they migrated from Rwanda many centuries ago. In this moment, his words are a machete that cuts me to the core. I feel empty, as though the part of me that's most substantial has gone, leaving me hollow. Only skin and bone.

My hand goes limp and slowly falls from my ear until finally the phone hits the carpeted floor. I can still hear Father, but his voice is now muffled and distant, reaching me as though through a tunnel. I lower myself into the dining chair that has found a permanent place by my living room window. I finger the cowrie shell necklace around my neck, wishing to go back in time before having this knowledge, back in time when I felt whole.

Time passes and it doesn't. Father's faraway voice through the phone stops, and silence eclipses the room. How long have I been sitting here, lost? He'll be worried, want to know I can be strong.

I hear the ping of email arriving. It's from Father. Kaaka went missing the evening before, and when she didn't return by nightfall, he put together a search party. A game ranger found her body lying among the moss under a tree canopy behind the waterfalls.

"It was lucky he found the body when he did, before some wild animals got to it. That would have been gruesome," Father's email says. I wonder about the moment my Kaaka became "the body." Did it hurt? Or was it peaceful?

Outside, the dark clouds have huddled closer together, blocking out the sun. Then slanted lashes of rain beat down from the sky, battering my windowpane like they want in to the apartment.

I pull on my sneakers and fly down the stairs, a caged bird let loose. I run toward Wascana Lake, a path shown to me by Mr. Stevenson. Gaining speed, I part grey sheets of rain as hot tears run down my cheeks. Every few minutes, bolts of lightning fire up the black skies, followed by a ripping sound like a great big cloth being torn down the seam. I splash through silver puddles pooling on the concrete lip of the lake. I want so badly to go back home.

"I'll have more tea," Kaaka says on the evening before I leave for Canada. But when I refill her cup, she sets it on the tree stump behind her, next to the kerosene lantern radiating amber light into the dusk. She fishes a lilac satin bag from the deep pocket of her tunic and presses it into the palm of my hand.

"Hold on to these for me, will you?"

The bag's contents clink together as I loosen the string tie to reveal cowries, their porcelain surfaces gleaming like sea-polished rocks. Kaaka stretches herself out on the mat, looking up into the stars as though she hasn't just offered me an everlasting memory. This ninety-year-old woman who raised me would have given me the shells on the night of my wedding to wish upon my marriage the strength of the Indian Ocean. Except I haven't brought a suitor home, and, at thirty years old, I've turned into an old maid.

"Have you also given up on me ever getting married, Kaaka?"

"Not at all," she says, still looking up into the indigo sky dotted with millions of stars, her hands forming a pillow underneath her cloud of grey hair. "I know you will get married. This is just my way of telling you that your worth isn't tied to marriage and procreation."

I try to undo the knot in the necklace I wear, the one I inherited from Mother after she died, but it won't loosen. It seems to have become tighter as the years have gone by. I keep tugging and pulling until eventually it loosens and comes apart. Mother had only six cowries on her necklace. Adding my new six makes it fuller, heavier. I'll be an old maid with twelve cowries around my neck, which is rare.

The light from the lantern makes shadows of the wrinkles in Kaaka's mahogany face. Lying there on the mat, she looks solemn, as if trying to untangle knots from an old memory. I'm struck by how tiny she is, how little space she takes up on our mat. She reminds me of a stub of a pencil worn with its work, the best of its years shaved away.

My mother was a dressmaker. In my head, I have an image of her sitting behind her sewing machine on the front porch of our cabin, a yellow pencil sticking out from behind her ear. As the pencils shrunk, she'd shove them into her puffy hair. I always imagined the tiny pencils getting lost in that thick hair, getting trapped in its tangles, no way out. I wanted to save them, but Mother never let me touch her hair.

"I can't remember her face," I say, lying down beside Kaaka. "Mother's face. The contours of it have faded." The realization, saying it out loud, hurts my chest. What kind of a daughter forgets her mother's face?

"You're the spitting image of her," Kaaka says. "Look into a mirror anytime and hers is the face that looks back at you. You have her voice, too. Sometimes I hear you speak and I think, Holy Stars! My daughter lives inside my granddaughter."

I was eight years old when Mother succumbed to the poison of a black mamba. That's when Kaaka came to live with Father and me. (Grandfather had left her years before to go live with a much younger woman.) On the day of my mother's funeral, Kaaka told me that Nyabingi, the rain goddess our tribe worships, had called Mother into the spirit world. She wanted me to understand that my mother still lived on, only now her physical presence was lost to us. I didn't tell her that her explanation was cruel, that it only made it harder for me to grieve for my mother.

"Tell me again how she died," I say, willing myself to accept her view of death, that it births one into a form of oneself bigger than life and visible only to the living whose eyes have grown eyes.

"You know how it happened. If you still have to ask, it means you doubt."

I'm a primatologist. I believe in verifiable, quantifiable data and logical explanations of the world. I was born in a cabin on the edge of a river, and I see connections everywhere. I bridge between species, places, and time. I was six years old when I first learned the names of all the birds in our sanctuary, from the little bronze mannikin to the imposing shoebill. I wrote them down in a notebook and recited them to tourists from Europe and North America like a morning prayer. I was ten when a baby chimpanzee hooted and purred his way into my heart. When we found him, Father and me, he still clung to his dead mother's leg. A poacher had shot her and left her for dead. It was then that I decided to study non-human primates, to try to protect them from humans.

"But how do you know for certain that Nyabingi took her? How do you know if Nyabingi exists?" I hear myself ask Kaaka.

"Because her spirit has visited me every night since she passed on. That's how I know."

This is brand new information. I don't know how to respond to it so I lie there quietly, too many questions hanging in the air above me.

The day after Mother's funeral, Kaaka packed a picnic. She sat me down by the river and said, "Repeat after me: My mother has been ushered into the spirit world."

I repeated the phrase because she'd told me to, not because I believed it.

"Say it with conviction," she pleaded. "I'm certain of it the way I know that the moon is the moon and the sun is the sun."

I wanted to believe her. Really, I did. But when the customary week of mourning ended and I returned to school, I told anyone who asked that a snake that moves faster than most people can run, whose venom is so potent and fast-acting that only two drops of it paralyzes its victims, killing them within an hour, that has a head the shape of a coffin and a mouth blacker than the chimney of a kerosene lantern, struck my mother twice. Trying to get away from this snake, she fell into the nameless river that runs through the sanctuary, and the river spat her out at its frothy mouth, where it feeds the swamp. That's more or less what Father had told me. The rest I had read in his big book on snakes of East Africa.

"Our dead are always with us," Kaaka is saying now. There's a hint of suppressed anger in her voice. "You must always remember this."

"I know but—"

"Why is it impossible for you to believe in a world whose existence you can't explain?" Kaaka speaks over my objection. "You are smart enough to know that just because you can't see something that doesn't mean it's not there."

A sort of electric hush charged with the loud singing of crickets sits between us. In the distance it creates, I probe the walls of Kaaka's theory of death, walls that are warped and distorted and never hold up whenever subjected to reason. But I suppose gods don't listen to reason. I suppose gods go about doing whatever they want even if it means leaving a trail of orphaned children and childless mothers.

"She just materializes at the foot of my bed like an image from a projector," Kaaka says. It takes me a moment to realize she's talking about Mother's spirit. "Except it's obviously not just an image because she tidies up in my room. She walks around picking my tunics from the floor and folding them and putting them away in my wardrobe."

"No!"

"She talks to me, too. It's a kind of wordless communication, like the hum of the forest. It took me a while to understand it, but now I do."

I want to ask her what else Mother has told her, but I don't. If she wants to, she will tell me unbidden. And after a moment's silence she does. Kaaka wants me to know that Mother's spirit has promised to escort her over to the other side soon, very soon. She wants me to be prepared for this possibility. I'm not to worry, though, she warns. I'm not to cry. This is the ending she desires. It's what she's always hoped for. I should want it for her.

"Will you come back and visit me?" I say, all of my sensible questions having deserted me. "When Mother takes you, will you come back to me?"

"If you want me to."

I don't know how long I've been running when a dog's bark stops me short in a dimly lit back alley. He's a large, black dog with a rumpled coat like the skin of an elephant. A white picket fence overrun with vines separates us. He scratches at it with his paws before giving up and turning away from me.

The rain has let up, but I'm still dripping wet, cold to the bone. I resume running to generate warmth. A bearded man with a long whip of braided hair down his back is standing outside a convenience store. He yells his sexual desires at me in an alcohol-induced drawl. I run. When we are scared, time slows. I'm running so fast it feels as if I'm standing still and everything around me is a blur. It seems incredible to me now that an hour or so ago I thought staying in my apartment one second longer might kill me. And now that I've strayed too far and don't know how to get back, I want, more than anything, the safety of its concrete walls.

I see a street sign up ahead, Cameron Street. The houses

on it look alike, old and eccentric. I run to the closest one and ring the bell by its purple door. My heart is beating sorely against my ribs. My throat is burning.

"I'm lost," I tell the middle-aged woman who opens the door. Waves of chocolate-coloured hair frame her long face. "May I use your phone to call a cab?"

"Come in, come in," she says, pulling the door wide open. Then, looking up a narrow staircase, she shouts, "Ganapati!" Her accent is East Indian. Her body emanates warmth and the sweet smell of jasmine. She offers me a large towel from a linen closet.

A younger man comes down the creaking stairs wearing a frown on his face. His white slacks are folded up at the bottom like someone at the beach who wants to wade into the water without getting their clothes wet. When he sees me, he tilts his head at a questioning angle.

"Weren't you about to leave?" the woman asks him, but she doesn't wait for his answer. "Can you drive this young woman to her home so she won't be swindled by a cab driver? Their fees are exorbitant, aren't they?"

I nod my head yes, even though I've never taken a cab.

The man introduces himself. He says I can call him Ganesh.

I put his name on my tongue, toss it around my mouth, and push it out between my teeth. I once knew a man with the same name. Ganesh. He stayed in one of our guest cabins at the sanctuary for three months. He wrote poems in jagged cursive all day long. In between bouts of writing, he walked around on calloused feet, touching Kaaka's honeysuckles, cutting his fingers on her roses, sucking up the little beads of blood. In the evenings, he sat cross-legged outside the cabin and recited his day's work. Kaaka and I listened to him in blissful incomprehension.

I shake Ganesh's hand, and a symphony surges through my brain. His face glows as though he's lit from within. My body is in love with him, this stranger named for a god. It bends toward him like a vining plant to light.

"I love your necklace," he says.

"Thank you. The cowrie shells are a gift from my grandmother Harriet. I'm named for her. My name is Harriet."

"A beautiful name."

Ganesh opens the passenger door of his blue sedan for me. He turns a corner onto 13th Avenue, and soon we are cruising down Albert Street. The shimmering surface of Wascana Lake is lit with fiery shades of gold and red. Where did I lose my way along this lake? Can we outrun fate?

"Here we are," he says, pulling up in front of my apartment building. "I'll walk you to the door."

I want to tell him that he needn't. That, contrary to prevailing evidence, I'm quite normal. That running too far and getting lost was really the universe's doing, not mine. But I hear how alien this self-defence sounds in my head, how lacking in logic, and I let him walk me to the entrance of my building.

We stand at the door and I awkwardly fumble around my wet pants, feeling for which one of its many pockets hides the key. Finding it, I hold it up victoriously, evidence that I'm not crazy, not completely. But mad people probably think that they are the normal ones—everyone else is insane and should get help.

"I better get going then," he says. But he doesn't leave. We stand at the door as though held together by something outside of ourselves.

"Would you like to come in?" I ask.

"Sure. But I can't stay long."

Inside my apartment, Ganesh offers me the details of his life like a present. He left India five years ago to attend a music residency at the Regina Conservatory of Performing Arts, and then he decided to stay afterwards. Now he's a pianist with the local symphony orchestra. The woman is his aunt. She owns an Indian restaurant downtown, and he dines with her every Sunday. Would I like him to make us some tea? What kind of tea do I have?

"Lemongrass. I have dry lemongrass." I pull open a kitchen cabinet to find it. "I brought it from home in Ziploc bags. In cut-up bits. An airport security officer wanted to toss them into a garbage can."

"Why?" Ganesh says, his hazel green eyes wide with surprise.

"He was worried I might try to plant 'whatever this stuff is' on Canadian soil."

Ganesh's laughter is the warm colour of hope. I excuse myself to change out of my wet clothes. When I return to the kitchen, Ganesh is tossing a fistful of lemongrass into a pan with water. As the lemongrass boils, its fragrance fills my apartment with the sweet smell of home. I close my eyes and inhale its aroma, remembering a time so recent yet so irretrievably gone.

Ganesh takes a sip of the tea and purses his lips; the taste hasn't lived up to his expectations. He sets the cup down on the kitchen counter and scribbles his phone number in my day planner that I left open after breakfast.

"You'll call me?" he asks.

"I will."

"You promise?" His high-pitched voice sounds like pleading.
"I do."

On the morning I leave for Canada, Kaaka puts her hand on
my back and leaves it there as she accompanies me to my
father's beat-up Range Rover, caked with mud. We stand on
the passenger side. I drape myself around her small frame,
breathing her in, letting her clean scent—the smell of soap
just unwrapped from its package—cleanse all the fissures of
my soul. I transform my body into a plaster mould and imprint
her on it, creating an impression of her on me.

"Christmas will come quickly," she whispers. "We'll see
each other very soon."

When she lets go of me, I have a sinking feeling, like I have
fallen out of time.

I'm sitting in my living room drinking the tea Ganesh abandoned. Without sugarcane syrup, it's bland, like a cheap,
watered-down version of the real thing. But the aroma is
potent and breathing it is restful.

I sink deeper into the couch, dropping my head over the
backrest like someone getting their hair washed in a salon.
And that's when I feel it—a hand on my shoulder. The sensation is real enough for me to jump up, terrified, but all I see
behind the couch is an unadorned wall the colour of dry bone.
And yet my shoulder carries a memory of the hand, its familiar
smallness and warmth. Suddenly, I'm filled with a lightness of
spirit and aware of the irreplaceable joy of this moment, what
it might mean. Are my eyes growing eyes? I'm open to all that
is possible.

CARLY VANDERGRIENDT

RESURFACING

The volunteers wait in a cluster on the beach. Thirty or so of them in all. Faces Jackie recognizes, people who've been coming to the Point for a long time. If her mother were here, she'd be nudging her and whispering, *That twit brings his wife up one weekend and his mistress the next.* Or, *Boy, did the DeWitt girl ever straighten out.*

The afternoon sun spills across the surface of the lake. You wouldn't know a man drowned here this morning. An out-of-towner. It's always the out-of-towners, thinks Jackie. They don't know about the rip current. It pulls you halfway to Erie, Pennsylvania, before you even realize.

"His poor family. How terrible," says Anna. A ladybug lands on her bare shoulder. She flicks it away.

What does Anna know about terrible things? Jackie wonders, glaring. There's a dull ache in her forehead, tucked behind her skull. She was trying to sleep it off when the helicopter started up. It circled for hours. She knew what it meant. After lunch, she told Chris to take their boys to town for the afternoon. Her brother, Jeff, went with them. Anna stayed.

Someone from Norfolk County Fire & Rescue had been by the cottage. A kayaker had gone missing that morning, he told Jackie. They needed help with the search.

The same county volunteer now reappears before the crowd, holding a loudspeaker. "We're going to make a chain," he calls, corralling them.

The group thins out. Anna seizes Jackie's right hand before she can move away. The lady who ends up on her left has a cottage on the channel side. Jackie thinks she was at her mother's funeral.

The county volunteer wades out to a Sea-Doo and revs the engine. He holds the loudspeaker in front of his face, calling them forward.

It's a slow march into the water. Jackie's arms break out in a rash of goosebumps. The lake is always colder after a storm. And opaque. Brown. Unsettled.

"I kind of hope we don't find him," whispers Anna. "Is that bad?"

"Don't think about it," says Jackie. Though she's thought about it herself. What it might feel like. The waterlogged body. She imagines a certain leadenness, pickled skin. She shivers.

They reach the first sandbar and stagger to a collective stop. Jackie is stretched between Anna and the woman from across the channel. Gentle waves slosh at her knees.

"We're stopping?" Anna pokes her head out and looks down the line.

The last time the Van Leeuwens came to the Point as a family, Jackie was fifteen. Later that year, her dad disappeared.

He was gone nine months before he reappeared like it was nothing. He wouldn't say where he'd been. Jackie's mother never got over it.

It probably killed her. But that came later.

Another call from the loudspeaker and they advance in slow motion. A line of lumbering astronauts. The water is up to Jackie's hips. This is where it drops off, she thinks.

"That's six to four," said Jackie. Smug, because she and Anna were winning. She pushed the cards toward Chris. "Your deal."

Chris didn't care for euchre. Not like the Van Leeuwens. They were a euchre-playing family. That is, when they were still a family. Their mother had been dead now for over a year. Neither Jackie nor Jeff spoke to their father. In fact, they only saw each other once a year, when Jackie and Chris brought the kids down from the Ottawa Valley.

"Time out," said Jeff. "Anyone want anything?"

"Another beer," said Chris.

"I'll take a top-up," Jackie said, handing Jeff her glass.

"Nothing for me," said Anna. She rose from the table and walked to the row of windows at the back, looking out at the shifting darkness that was the lake.

"You sure?" called Jackie. All of the windows were shut, but the sound of the roaring wind and crashing waves filled the cottage.

Anna didn't answer.

Jackie tried to exchange an eye-roll with Chris, but he was caught up dealing the next hand. On his face, the same look of forced concentration Cole made when he read. She smiled at the thought of their eldest son. Buoyed by two glasses of white wine and several rum and cokes, she could forget the fight he'd put up about brushing his teeth. And Felix, her sweet baby. Maybe he wouldn't cry for her later on that night. Alcohol made raising kids seem only mildly awful.

Chris doled out four neat piles of five cards. He put the kitty in the middle of the table and turned over the top card.

"Not yet," whispered Jackie. "Jeff'll murder you."

He turned the card back over. Under the table, she rubbed a clumsy foot against his. God, she loved him. For stepping in when Cole got mouthy. For playing euchre. For making an effort with Jeff and his fun-sponge of a girlfriend. Anna wouldn't even have a drink, now what was that about? She was too thin to be pregnant. When Jeff brought her last year, Jackie hadn't paid much attention because Jeff's relationships never lasted. He didn't even have a type. Women, plural. That used to be his type.

Jackie studied Anna as she returned to the table. Tall and gawky, with that thing all the twenty-something women were talking about. A thigh gap. Jackie's thighs were dimpled and doughy, like *oliebollen* batter. They probably hadn't *not* touched since 1988.

"Windy out there," said Anna.

"Gearing up for a storm," said Jeff. He smiled, set the drinks on the table, and took his seat next to Jackie. Jeff wasn't some megastud, thought Jackie. He was just a likeable guy. He should have been bored with Anna by now.

"Erie likes to show off," Jackie added. A distant clap of thunder sounded, as if to prove her point.

"I guess that's our cue," said Chris. "Game on."

"Yes, sir," said Jeff.

Chris turned over the upcard. They lifted their cards to their chests. For a second, Jackie imagined Jim-and-Janet and Jeff-and-Jackie circa 1982. Bound to each other by some invisible force, they sat in the shadowy living room of the cottage, playing out yet another summer storm.

Jackie had a dismal hand. Three nines, two queens, and only one of every single suit. She passed. The others did too. Jeff and Chris took five tricks that hand, tying the game six-six. It was Jackie's turn to deal.

"Do you remember," started Jeff, "when Mom used to go away for the weekend and we'd stage those euchre tournaments in the basement?"

Now, whenever they were together, they ended up reminiscing about that parentless time. Adulthood had set Jeff and Jackie adrift of one another. That parentless time was all they had.

"Marty lost his old junker in a bet," said Jackie, as she dealt the cards. "And on Monday morning his dad showed up at school to beg Jerry De Vries to give it back."

"Where was your mom?" asked Anna.

Jackie bristled as she turned over the queen of spades.

"Our dad left," Jeff explained. Not missing or lost. Just left. As if the real leaving came then and not later. "When he left, she would go around to different cities showing his picture to people."

"She just left you two alone?" asked Anna. White lightning filled the cottage, illuminating the freckles on her nose.

"It was the '80s," said Jeff. "Things were different then."

"To be fair," Jackie cut in, "Jeff was seventeen. He should have been capable of looking after me. Instead he started an illegal gambling operation in our basement."

"Well, what about that babysitter Mom hired?" asked Jeff. "She wasn't exactly going out of her way to stop me. Pass, by the way."

Jeff always brought up the babysitter, Jackie thought. Did he know? She studied her hand. She had both bowers. If she picked up that queen, she could go this round alone. That'd be four points and a win for her team. That'd show Jeff.

"She was nineteen," said Jackie.

"Pass," said Anna.

"Pass," said Chris, his eyes on his cards. "What was her name again?"

"Sharon," said Jackie, off-handedly. "Spades." She picked up the queen. "I'm going to go it alone."

Anna sighed as she set her cards face down on the table.

"Winner gets the loser's car," said Jeff, playing the ace of diamonds. Chris followed suit with a jack.

"You want our minivan?" asked Jackie, taking the trick. "You can have it."

"You know she was at Mom's funeral."

"Who?"

"Sharon."

"I know," snapped Jackie. Seeing Sharon at the funeral had sparked a small-scale, pre-midlife crisis during which Jackie began compulsively noticing women. There was Cole's teacher, a sinewy woman with a mop of tight brown curls. There was the blond woman from the Office of External Relations with the New Agey name Jackie could never remember. What did Jackie like? She had no clue. Once, she had liked Sharon.

"She looked different," said Jeff. "Don't you think?"

"I'd hope. Twenty years later," said Jackie. What was he getting at? "Look. Can we, like, drop the babysitter thing?"

"I thought you guys were friends?"

"Why would I be friends with our old babysitter?"

She slapped the left bower down. Jeff laid a low spade, Chris an ace. Jackie took the trick. Three more tricks and she'd get her four points. She looked at Anna, who was sitting with her chin propped on her hands, a yawn about to slide across her face.

"You were so close back then."

"Are you still friends with everyone from back then?" Wrong question, Jackie knew immediately. Jeff had never left their hometown.

"Don't get so worked up." Her brother was the only person in the world who could use that line. And it worked. Now, she couldn't deny being worked up without sounding worked up. Jackie had a thought, then. A boozy thought. What if she told him?

She played the right bower. "You know what?" she started.

"What?" asked Jeff, laying down an off-suit card.

Chris hesitantly showed diamond. Jackie took her third trick.

"Sharon and I—" continued Jackie. She had to play a card first. King of spades or king of clubs? She chose the spade.

"Yes?"

"We were girlfriends." No, thought Jackie. That wasn't right. Not girlfriends—she has girlfriends now. Female friends, that is. "We were . . . together."

"What?"

"We were," she hesitated, "romantic."

Jeff scrunched his brow. He set the jack of diamonds down. Chris played a nine, and Jackie took a fourth trick. She lifted her chin as she swept up the cards, noticing Anna was staring at her.

"You were, what, fifteen? Isn't that kind of wrong?" Jeff paused. "She took advantage of you."

"Right," said Jackie. At the funeral, the four years between them seemed utterly insignificant. "Because you never dated anyone that young when you were nineteen."

Another clap of thunder sent the plates clinking in the cupboards. Felix would be awake soon, thought Jackie. She played her last card.

"That's different," said Jeff. "I mean, at that age. How could you know?" He played a low diamond and looked to Chris. "Did you know about this?"

"What does it have to do with him?" asked Jackie. She heard a moan from the boys' room.

"Yeah," Chris answered, clutching his last card. "I knew."

"And it doesn't bother you?"

"Why would it?" asked Chris. He set the card down. The ace of clubs. So Chris had the ace. He took the trick as Felix erupted into a full-fledged wail.

"Then I guess everything worked out," said Jeff, looking from Jackie to Chris and back. He swiped the cards into a messy pile. "What is that now? Seven to six?"

Jackie frowned. "What's that supposed to mean?"

"It means you didn't get your four points," said Jeff.

"No," said Jackie. "You guess everything worked out? You mean I didn't end up with Sharon? You mean I'm not—" Jackie stopped herself. She stood up and left the table.

The darkness in the boys' room was disorienting. "Mummy's here," she whispered. She padded her way to the bottom bunk and fit her body next to Felix's, lifting his pyjama to rub the hot skin on his back. "Shhh," she murmured.

Sharon had left for university around the same time Jackie's father reappeared. For months, Jackie wrote her long-winded letters in blue ink, the ballpoint tip tearing through the paper while her mother's voice spilled from the family room, husky and bitter. *Tell me. Where did you go?* But Jackie never heard a response.

Eventually, Sharon stopped writing back.

After a few minutes, Jackie could feel her son's small body letting go, his awareness receding. His breathing slowed. She wouldn't be like her own mother. She wouldn't abandon her children before they were ready.

Jackie got over Sharon. She moved to Ottawa to go to university, where she met Chris. She married and thought little of the past. Her father's disappearance and his refusal to talk about it had wedged itself like a stake between the members of the Van Leeuwen family. Her parents divorced, and Jackie had her own kids. When her mother got sick, she found she wanted to tell her about Sharon. She wanted to say, *This is what was happening then, and you had no idea.*

But she didn't.

Jackie hadn't realized she'd dozed off until the door opened. There was someone in the doorway.

"Chris?" she muttered.

From the bed, Jackie saw the hall light silhouetting Anna's thighs, the space between them glowing. She sat up, startled.

⸺◦⸺

They're up to their midriffs now, their linked hands suspended above the surface. Jackie looks back. The pastel-coloured cottages are strung out like beads on a candy necklace.

"I wonder," says Anna, "how much farther we can walk."

"Erie is shallow," says Jackie. "There's a second sandbar." They used to make it that far as kids. Then their mother would stand on the beach and holler into the wind for them to come in. Because that's what mothers are supposed to do, and that's what Jackie's mother had always done. Until her husband left and she just stopped. Hollering. Caring.

"What I don't get," starts Anna, "is how a full-grown man gets pulled under here.

"That's it," says Jackie. "The current doesn't pull you under. It pulls you out. You get tired. And then—"

"Oh," says Anna.

"It happens every year."

"You mean, people drown?"

"Yeah."

"Jeff never mentioned that."

"Mr. Positive," says Jackie.

"I know."

Jackie waits for her to say more.

"Jeff is great."

"Yeah?"

"It's just . . . I don't know if he told you? But I'm on an antidepressant. It makes me kind of. Not myself," says Anna.

Is she talking about last night? wonders Jackie.

"It's like. Sometimes I do things and I just don't care about the consequences."

Jackie was still foggy with sleep when Anna sat down on the bed. Her hand grazed Jackie's leg, ever so lightly. Jackie's heat felt like shame, her son sleeping next to her in the bed. She stood up. Dizziness caught her as Anna left the room.

The water laps at her collarbone. Around them, the chain is breaking. The lady from the channel side lapses into a doggie paddle. Jackie pulls her hand from Anna's, lifts her feet from the sandy bottom. That's when she sees it. A flash of something pale between the waves. Driftwood, thinks Jackie, because dead bodies don't float. Or do they?

"Can you see that?"

"What?" asks Anna. Her head is still above the water, her feet still planted.

"There's something there." Treading, Jackie points. The more she studies it, the more it looks like a limb. An arm, maybe.

"I see it," says Anna.

Jackie kicks. Her foot jabs at sand. It's getting shallower. She can stand again.

"Come forward," calls the county volunteer.

They walk until they hit an incline. The second sandbar. The water level drops to their ribs now. Jackie keeps her eyes fixed on the floating thing. If it's actually part of a body, wouldn't the helicopter have spotted it, protruding from the water like that? It catches the sunlight, slick and shining.

"Stop. Let's reform the chain."

Anna extends her hand. Jackie hesitates, takes it.

"Should we say something?" asks Anna.

Before Jackie can answer, they're moving forward again. It's just a piece of wood, she tells herself. Likely blew in with the storm. So why isn't it drifting closer? It disappears, resurfacing in the same place, about twenty feet away, a moment later.

She finds herself thinking about the man. *His poor family.* Are his loved ones out searching? There are times when she wishes her own father had stayed lost. Her mother would have called off the search. Fifteen feet now. She is almost sure—it isn't. Him. But the way it moves. Fluid-like. Not bobbing. Not like driftwood. Ten feet. Jackie tightens her grip on Anna's hand. The women on either side tug her along until she stops, digging her heels into the sand. The chain bows around her. At last, she sees the illusion. It's just a branch. A piece of driftwood masquerading as a man's arm.

GREG BROWN

LOVE

We agreed as a family that the only thing to do was to bring Mom home for the next few months or weeks, whatever it would be. It'll be hard, Dad said. But maybe it can be fine, too. Denisa was suspicious about the cost of it all—like the private nurse we'd have to pay for, where at the hospital it was free—although she didn't put it like that, said that we'd be crazy to bring Mom into a place where there wasn't any immediate care, because what if there was a problem like before, the thing with her stent that plugged up and caused some internal bleeding that almost wasn't staunched in time?

She *could've*, Denisa said.

The oncologist had said October, and the late pale fog had come and now the sky was mostly dimmed and gone by suppertime.

I said that I would only do it if we agreed that Pastor Karen would not come to the house; I was not comfortable with

Pastor Karen coming to the house. Jon and Dad looked at me a moment and said, Okay.

Denisa said, I don't get what you don't like about Pastor Karen.

And I explained why I didn't like Pastor Karen.

And Denisa said, Well, I don't think it's really fair to call her a liar.

And I explained why I thought it was fair to call Pastor Karen a liar.

And Denisa said, Well, by that standard they're all liars. And then we'd all be liars, too. The whole thing would be a lie. We don't need lies right now.

And I agreed with Denisa, especially about how we didn't need lies right now.

And Denisa said, It doesn't matter, because who cares what we know and don't know. If Mom wants her to visit, then she visits.

I said, I care.

And Denisa said, You're unbelievable.

The family counsellor in the palliative care ward arranged for the hospital to loan us one of their extra beds, and then one of the RNs in the palliative care ward arranged for a delivery service to bring the bed by and for the ambulance service to drive Mom from the hospital. We watched, standing far clear of the foyer, uncertain about how wide a berth to give, as the ambulance attendants bounced the gurney over the uneven tile in the kitchen.

You're home, Dad said, as the attendants rolled Mom from the gurney into the special hospital bed. Mom looked up and smiled and didn't say anything.

She passed very early the next morning, and Dad woke us

up to tell us what had happened. That he'd gone into her room to help her with her bedpan and that he'd found her very still, nothing going into her and nothing coming out. I don't know why he said it like that: "Nothing going into her and nothing coming out." Then he said that he'd already called the hospital and spoken with Dr. Halford and that Dr. Halford said that the hospital would send over the ambulance and he reminded Dad about the paperwork that he would need to have at hand because the coroner would also be over with the ambulance because it was protocol for the coroner to check in to make sure that we had the right kind of permits for the deceased. I don't know why Dad told us all of this, we didn't need to know it.

There isn't a lot of time, Dad said, before they'll be here to take her, and I think you should each take a moment.

We would take turns sitting with the body in the bedroom—if it was just that, a body—where it was still prone in the borrowed hospital bed, where nothing was going into it and nothing coming out.

First, it was Jon's turn since he was the youngest and that seemed fair and important to honour. The rest of us sat in the living room where we hadn't yet taken down the Christmas decorations and listened, but also did not listen, to the sounds that were coming out of the bedroom. We looked at the Christmas tree because there was nothing else to look at and because it was there and because we'd forgotten to take it down. We'd done a very good job decorating it, even though we'd used many homemade decorations—gingerbread men with purple silk looped through their head-holes and chains of old popcorn threaded with green fishing line. I don't like homemade decorations because they look sloppy and cheap and often like they are made by children, as these ones were, since of course we'd made them as children many, many years ago. But I thought the tree looked almost fine.

We could hear Jon speaking, but I tried not to hear it and I clenched my jaw just tightly enough to aggravate the ringing in my left ear. But the tree looked fine even with the ringing in my ear and Jon's quiet noises, and my only real regret about the tree was the winged, brass treetopper—which actually was store-bought, not handmade by us as children—which was canted at the top of the tree either because the last tree spoke or whatever you call the top branch was bent or because Jon, who'd been the one to put it on top of the tree, had put it on in a hurry, although that didn't seem very likely, he was careful mostly.

Jon came out and he was wiping his nose with the collar of his shirt. He sat down beside Dad, and Dad put an arm around him and then they leaned their heads together, almost like they were in love.

Then Denisa stood up and said, There's no way.

And Dad said, You won't get another chance.

And Denisa said, I don't want to remember any of this. And then Denisa sat back down and covered her face with one of the Christmas throw pillows.

In the bedroom, there was the body still in the bed, nothing going into it. Her eyes shone brightly, still full of wet surprise and I wondered if she was *actually*. I stood beside the borrowed hospital bed that had been brought into our house and I stood and looked down at her, the body. There was nothing to do or to say. I remembered that before, when she was in the hospital, she wasn't always lucid. She dreamed while she was awake—that's how Dr. Halford explained it—and talked through the dreams as they appeared to her. I remembered that in one dream it was like she was a small child. It seemed like somebody was angry at her, like she'd done something wrong. I stood and listened for a while.

I won't say it, she said. It's poison to say it. Jon is sick because he said the words. He has a fever and I don't want to catch the fever. This school is a bad school. This school makes you sick if you say the words.

I became scared and left the room and found one of the nurses and told her what was happening. When we got back to the room she was still talking, but she seemed better.

Would you put another log on the fire, dear, Mom said. It's very cold.

The nurse said, Of course, darling, let me see what's left of the cord out back. And then Mom was quiet for a while and the nurse said to me, I hope you don't mind about that. And even though I was angry because I don't believe in lying, I didn't say anything.

And weeks later—she was in the hospital for so long—she woke up in the early evening and she said to me, Oh, there are angels outside the door. I hear them. They're saying that they're here for me. They're here to heal me. To make me better. They say that I'm cured. And I said, Mom, no. And she said, Open the door. And I said, Please, stop. And she said, You're not listening to me. The angels are here, you've got to let them in before they leave. Stop, I said. She said, You don't make them wait. And I said, Look, the door is open and where are the angels? She leaned out of her bed, wincing or searching

I couldn't say. Her body was so small and yellow and slow. She stared at the empty doorway and then lay back down. You're right, she whispered. There's nothing. I'm sorry.

It's fine, I said.

LIZ HARMER

NEVER PROSPER

One day, when Paul was practicing at one of the seven grand pianos in their winter home, the Palais Wittgenstein, he leaped up and shouted at his brother Ludwig in the room next door, "I cannot play when you are in the house, as I feel your skepticism seeping towards me from under the door."
—from Anthony Gottlieb's "A Nervous Splendor"

Of course there was no end to the cheaters. Evie prepared for the meeting by looking over the essay, which was so poorly cut-and-pasted that it contained several different font styles and sizes, and then the final sentence just ran off a cliff, no period, no final payoff to the opening promise: *After all it is clear that Wittgenstein believed.* She had now read the paper more times than it deserved, though it did have a strange beauty. *We have so far said nothing whatever*: a direct quote from the text itself but unattributed as such. Still, it was incredibly to the point.

She knew the name but not the face of the student who had produced such a mess. She had interacted with Steven Vandersteen only via email, emails that were also syntactically odd and sometimes even offensive in their illiteracy. *Be there at 3*, he had written, and despite the strange command of its phrasing, its keenness to keep her in this office chair, waiting, she knew that he really meant that *he* would be there at 3. She was sure she had never seen him. She knew the names of the twenty-seven who bothered to attend class regularly, and she knew the faces of those who never showed but sometimes came to her office hours as though their smiling manoeuvrings would earn them the grade they wanted. Steven Vandersteen, whose name had a performative quality as though invented for the sake of sound, belonged to a third category.

Teaching was a useless activity. Like torture as an interrogation technique, it did not produce the effect it was meant to. Torture never delivered the truth, and teaching never delivered knowledge, regardless of methodology. Evie's disillusionment was nearly complete. *I am receiving a salary*, she told herself. *I have an office and prestige.* Meanwhile the students received the grades they needed, learning nothing. Only those already inclined to understand something did. She swivelled in the chair she'd picked out in the office furniture catalogue in a swell of optimism in August, and looked out at the few bobbing palm leaves along the parking lot. She hated palm trees now more than ever.

Cheating did not give her hives, but she was required to investigate and perhaps to punish those who plagiarized or stole. As someone who had never cheated—who had not even taken a shortcut or skimmed a book!—Evie had the illogical intuition that the principles of order in the universe would justly punish such people with or without her intervention.

It was ten after three. Steven Vandersteen was late. She left all the windows on the monitor open, each of her papers an attempt to untwist an elaborate knot, like a cop in those detective shows pinning up photos and strings to connect them on a board. Instead of working, though, she logged in to Facebook, where she saw that Natasha had just posted a few photos of herself in Queen's Park, and near Robarts Library, and in front of the Humanities building. Toronto with its trees flaming into colour and the olive green scarf Natasha wore loosely over her sweater were autumnal, and homesickness pricked Evie. She clicked *Like* on the photos—they weren't selfies but there was no word on her companion—and then messaged Natasha: *Since when are you in TO?* Natasha seemed to be logged in but did not respond.

Natasha was the only one Evie could talk to about Tom. Evie had known him now for twelve years, since the Philosophy of Language class they'd both taken. He'd criticized her after the first session for nodding too much. "Your nodding does nothing to humanize you," he'd said outside the building in a drizzle, with a cigarette pinned to his mouth. His squint had a James Dean quality, but Evie thought she was immune to this, never having cared for James Dean. She blushed. Her nodding during class was a private movement cruelly exposed. To seem unperturbed she bummed a cigarette and smoked with him in the rain.

Later she discovered that she was exactly his type: straight blond hair, the body of a high-school athlete. He liked to make women blush; the other philosophy majors knew him well. The professor in that class, an eccentric whose glasses would often fly off his face by the force of his gesticulations, adored Tom. Tom got the only easy As in the class, drinking all night and then tossing off essays a few hours before class began in the dim lamplight of his dorm room desk, on a typewriter that he used instead of the computer labs like everybody else. Tom and that professor—Dr. de France—had a Wittgenstein/Russell dynamic. Bertrand Russell had once said of Wittgenstein admiringly that he was "destitute of the false politeness that interferes with truth."

For all her perky nodding, Evie really had to work in that class. Her notes included the sentences of encoded formal logic that Dr. de France scribbled on the chalkboard, muttering that the students wouldn't understand these but really they ought to be able to, and she sat there writing until her wrist hurt, hating de France and Tom both. Her ambition was as big as theirs was, but her naivety disguised her. That she liked Gottlieb Frege for asking the question they were all thinking: What is a number anyway? That she liked the verve of a philosopher called Quine, who said that if we see a person pointing at a rabbit and saying "gavagai," we don't know if "gavagai" means "rabbit" or "undetached rabbit part" or "time-slice of a rabbit," and to assume that their language disclosed the same conceptual scheme would be shameful, despite the silliness of the example. By then, she had become utterly conscious of her every movement in the class (Tom sat two rows over and one back, and she felt the heat of his looking at her on the back of her neck), and soon afterwards she was sleepless in his bunk listening to the anachronistic type-tapping of his genius through the night, the dings and rolling, the chatter of keys a soundtrack so particular to their romance that whenever she heard it she rushed with feeling for him, like a person accused of nodding stupidly.

Her only contact with him now was on Facebook or over text. Men believed themselves to be unsentimental, but they were the worst of all. Sometimes he would text her, just: *the present king of France is bald*. It was a reference to this class, where they'd met and first read these essays by Russell to do with truth-claims and sentences that seem to have no meaning. He would text it only if they hadn't talked in a while, and it meant: I miss you, don't forget about me.

So she and Natasha talked too much about him. Natasha had appeared in grad school the way a fairy does in a tale. Evie had followed Tom to U of T, and he'd acted surprised that she'd gotten in on the same level of scholarship that he had. His disdain was almost as good as being treated roughly in bed.

Natasha was dark-eyed and sleek with makeup, black hair long and shiny with care, and Evie was sure that Tom would sleep with her. Natasha's look of arrogant self-certainty and the intelligence in her eyes were, to him, nearly an invitation. A seminar they all took became an occasion for the two of them to engage in foreplay while Evie watched. Blowjobs came up as illustrations of Hegelian dynamics more than once. Evie prepared herself for it, expected to find them in his bed, or to find one of Natasha's scarves hanging over a piece of his furniture. It wasn't as though Evie and Tom were together; it wasn't as though she hadn't found out he was sleeping with another woman before. But for about a year, her heart would race every time she had her hand on a doorknob for fear of what lay behind it.

"I don't like women who try so hard," Tom told Evie when she brought up Natasha, early on.

Years later, Natasha said, "I don't know why you like him. He's not likeable."

"It's not that I like him. It's force. Animal attraction."

"You want to be pushed around, but you should find a better man than Tom to do it," Natasha said. Grad school didn't turn Natasha's looks; not only did she not go ragged but her nails were still done. Evie became wan and cowed, blond hair limp, going brittle like an old book.

Natasha was now living in Germany on a fellowship. They were geographically triangulated, one on either side of Tom and Toronto. Evie relished any contact with him, which, at this point, tended to be criticisms of her Facebook posts. He was a man who had come of age in the nineties and still thought like Kurt Cobain, or like Ethan Hawke's character in *Reality Bites*—that one's every action must be perfectly consistent if one is to have dignity. He still believed in the concept of selling out. Smiling at a customer at the Gap or at the Dean who might give you a job when you do not feel like smiling is thus a form of lying. It was a maddening but deeply attractive quality, though now that he was on Facebook he was disappointingly knowable. He always liked her pictures, always criticized her for complimenting someone else, and could be counted on to message her whenever she complained about Southern California. These were Tom bait—she posted such updates when she craved an argument with him.

I'm not obligated to find this place beautiful, she told him. *It's a desert.*

You have everything you ever wanted, he wrote. *It's ridiculous for you to complain.*

I don't have everything. And I'm entitled to my feelings.

You need someone, he wrote. *You're no good on your own.*

The gall of this man! But she knew that he only meant that he was lonely, that he was no good on his own, that he needed someone.

"Maybe he wants to live in the desert with you," Natasha said later, during their phone-call debriefs. "Or it's just Tom being Tom. Some men enjoy knowing that women are talking about them, calling them asshole."

(Tom had once called Natasha a "femme fatale.")

"I think he's just immature. But he won't be gorgeous forever."

"He has a man-bun," Natasha said. "And he knows exactly what he's doing."

3:18. Steven Vandersteen had not yet shown. Natasha had not replied to Evie's message but had replied to various fawning comments to her photos, all variations of "what a babe," with the obligatory "aw, you guys are sweet" in response. They all pretended that this wasn't the game, this vanity, that the photos' sole purpose wasn't to attract envy and admiration.

Evie should know. She had not become threatening but more attractive to men since winning the position. Men turned around her like spokes around a hub. She had started wearing daring shades of lipstick—reds and neon pinks—and to admire herself in reflective surfaces when she passed them. She could not distinguish the feeling of attraction from the feeling of being attractive, her desire from her vanity. The better things seemed to get the worse they were: this was the hard truth.

Ludwig Wittgenstein's prosperity was a curse. Three of his brothers committed suicide, while the fourth, a pianist, lost a hand. Ludwig threw himself into the battles of World War I, spent his life plagued by the puzzles of philosophy and by his fortune, which he kept trying to give away, an incurable virus of wealth. The Nazis came and the Wittgensteins fled. Between the wars, Ludwig abandoned the work that made him famous and moved north to teach schoolchildren. As a young man, his aptitudes had been mechanical and he had worked on hot-air balloons as an engineer. The schoolchildren tromped behind him in the woods while he told them the names for things. He was an expert whistler.

He worked as a medic during World War II and tried to avoid his fans. By then, a circle of believers had formed in Vienna around his philosophy, and he had earned the raving admiration of Bertrand Russell. Ludwig hit the schoolchildren with a ruler.

"About which one cannot speak thereof one must remain silent," he wrote in the trenches of World War I. All purists wish that a word was a clean window, a direct line. All purists like stillness and singularity. In the preface to his final work he expresses his frustration at his results being "variously misunderstood, more or less mangled or watered down." This "stung my vanity," he wrote. As for his vanity, he "had diffi-culty quieting it."

—

At least she liked her office. The palm trees were not so bad from afar, the vista a postcard cliché, though she had since learned from her landlord that they were full of rats. "They live in the palms, honey," he'd said after she saw a disheart-eningly large brown rodent on her balcony. "The palms are filled with 'em." Now she could see that their plaits of woven bark must be easy for a rodent to climb. And of course every-one talked about the smog. The dirty air—who knew on the particulate level what it really was?—blotted out, some days, all proof of mountains. Or created cotton candy skies at sunset.

Everyone back where it still snowed and rained in reason-able intervals believed she had won a jackpot, and now she needed to figure out how best to manage the envy of others. But Southern California was just like everywhere; people hated their lives here as they did everywhere else. She had opinions about the sky. Grey weather had not been the cause of her gloom, but had carried it like vapour. Gloom had a pres-sure system, too, and the blue sky was a taunt, cheerful as a sixties housewife. She longed for a downpour.

The glamour of philosophy, its sheen and its thrill, would soon dull for these students. It happened to everyone, except for madmen, maybe: the first dose of philosophy, which seems to question everything you thought you knew, is actually heady with illusions. A year or two of undergrad, three if you were lucky, and then you hit peak illusion, believing as you did that these thoughts mattered, that you were doing something both deep and important. But the end result was predeter-mined. What you thought was freedom landed you in an air-conditioned office somewhere, no better than a clerk. Type,

type, tap. A person struggled to get up a mountain and, well, you know the rest. You can tire of a view.

She now had to manage the students' illusions. Wittgenstein thrilled them because of his renegade personality. He was a Jesus figure, toppling tables. So she told them his biography, she laughed over *gavagai*, she said, "What, we may ask, is a number?" and she did not tell them when they came to her office for advice about switching their major to philosophy that you only ended up becoming a desk-jockey if you were one of the lucky ones. She would not say to them, Look, you are headed to loneliness. If you even get a job, you will have to move far away from everyone you love.

Tom had once told her that he adored her strangeness, but she thought he only found her strange because he was prejudiced against blond women. But, then, being a genius often makes a person an asshole, and she pointed this out in lectures when she wanted a laugh. During his tenure as an abusive schoolteacher, Ludwig wrote in a letter to Russell, "I am still at Trattenbach, surrounded, as ever, by odiousness and baseness."

3:23. She refreshed the feed. Nothing from Natasha, but a new photo from Tom. Tom Abstract (he had of course invented a bullshit name)—with Natasha Balay. It was a picture of the two of them fairly close up—definitely he was holding the phone that took the picture—in Queen's Park, surrounded by trees gone gold, dropping leaves in a glitter. Their faces were nearly touching. "Philosophers in Autumn," he'd titled it. She cringed at the attempt to be ironic that read as gravely sincere. They think that they're philosophers, she thought. It was like calling yourself a poet when you'd never published a thing. But after her cringe came another set of facial expressions, which she did not see in the reflection of her screen, because she was so focused on the photo. The *Likes* were pouring in. Someone had commented: *look how cute you are together.*

Eight months ago, she'd been checking into the hotel here and saw Tom coming out of an elevator with his duffle bag. She looked away, since she often hallucinated familiar faces while travelling, but he spotted her and came right to the front desk and watched the concierge give her a key. "It's a beautiful hotel," Tom said. "Quite a town."

The hotel was built to look like an old mission (she'd thought it was an actual converted mission and was not disabused of this until after she'd accepted the job), and the cool Mexican tiles alone were enough to convince a person that this would be a wonderful place to live.

"What are you doing here?"

They were frozen in the lobby, staring at each other. A breeze from the bronze, old-timey ceiling fans tossed his shoulder-length hair. He was looking craggier every year, long lines where his dimples used to be, eyes a bit bloodshot, though through the alchemy of his charm all of this made him seem more beautiful.

"Did you think you were the only big shot with a campus interview?"

It was then she understood what was meant by the phrase *I was floored.* She gathered herself and tossed back to him: "Oh, you have a secret interview. You must be taking this very seriously."

He liked it when she hit him with things she herself would have hated to hear. The meaner she was to him, the warmer he was to her. "Let's have a drink. I've got a few hours before I have to catch my flight." He led her to the bar, which, since it was the middle of the day, was mostly empty. She was still crumpled as the clothes in her suitcase. "Pretty soon they'll know everything about you," he said.

"Just like you do, I guess," she said.

"I do know everything about you."

She sipped her old fashioned through the tiny straw. "What do you think I want to do right now, if you're so smart?"

In the hotel room, in bed with him, she felt as she always had in all those years of letting this happen. It had happened a thousand times; it had been six months since the last time; it was always the same: just at their moment of greatest intimacy, his warm flesh against hers, absorbed by hers, his moaning and sighing marks of vulnerability, she felt that she could not trust him. His mouth was on her until she couldn't bear it, until she was almost in a trance, hallucinating a third party as though her suspicions were made flesh. So, now, against the door, lifted onto the bathroom counter, him pulling her open with his hands, and then on the bed, distrust flicked through her. "What are you doing?" she cried out as she came. He wanted to distract her before her interview.

"You romanticize my despair," he said. But the magic had gone out of him. In all those years, Evie hadn't slept with anyone else, as though a silent commitment could stand in for monogamy. He said, "Let the best man win," before letting himself out the door, and she nodded, decided that though he'd hoped to throw her off her game she'd use the fuck to her advantage. She was desirable, powerful, the sort of person who could shake off an intense encounter and go into a room full of strangers and charm them with her poise.

"Whatever you do, don't drink, no matter how much you want to," her advisor had told her. She downed a black coffee and then another. She rinsed out her mouth with tepid water and brushed her teeth. She zipped on her nicest pencil skirt.

Now it was Evie who'd started drinking. She was not an alcoholic and could admit that she was drinking excessively, watching bad reality TV and *Dr. Phil* and going through a twenty-sixer of Wild Turkey every week. This is not the outcome we expected, she thought he'd say if he were here with her and not with Natasha in Toronto. Now it was Evie who was drinking and Tom who was in love. There was a language to these photos. She knew it was post-coital and then also pre-coital. Now, 3:29, Natasha had finally replied. *Yes! I'm in Toronto!* Then, *How are you?*

Go fuck yourself, Evie thought, trembling like a palm. Before she could think better of it, below the photo of the two of them, she copy-and-pasted a quote from the lecture she'd been writing. "*I know that human beings are on the average not worth much anywhere, but here they are more good-for-nothing and irresponsible than elsewhere.*" Take that! The slim moment of triumph was followed by terror, but before she could figure out how to delete it, Steven Vandersteen walked in.

Well, it turned out that Steven Vandersteen wore a top hat. She was in no mood to laugh, and, trembling still, Evie looked calmly at the hat and the bearded face beneath it and gestured at the chair for him to sit.

"I assume you are Steven Vandersteen," she said. "Nice to finally meet you."

He smirked at her. Then, he lifted his finger and thumb to the brim of the hat and tipped it at her. "Likewise."

"So, I've got your essay here, and I just wanted to consult with you before I send it down the channels."

"Yeah."

"I mean, you didn't write this, right?"

"I wrote it."

"You arranged it."

"If you think about it," he said, with such an emphasis that it was clear he thought she hadn't thought about it, "that's all every essay is. An arrangement of various invented words."

"I have to disagree with that," she said.

"There is nothing new under the sun. Who said that?"

She stared at him. Men always taking it upon themselves to teach her.

"Marcus Aurelius," he said.

"Actually, it's from the Book of Ecclesiastes."

"I can guarantee you," he said, seeming not to have heard her, "that Wittgenstein wouldn't care one way or another whether he received attribution. He was purely interested in the truth."

He pronounced the *W* in *Wittgenstein* as a *W*, and for a moment she felt sorry for him. He was the sort of kid who thought that genius was worth something, the sort of kid who wants to find out that he is a genius, or, rather, the sort of kid who is certain that he is a genius and is just waiting for someone to discover it. Like a tall, thin woman waiting for a modelling agent to come along.

"You never come to class, and you've committed several shades of academic dishonesty. Not just misattribution but outright plagiarism. And regardless of the possibility for novelty on this Earth, there are rules and consequences in the university, and—"

"Man, I feel sorry for you," he said.

She was still trembling. She took a deep breath. "What are your plans? I saw that you're a philosophy major."

"Yep."

"Well, you're wasting your money and your time if you don't bother learning the ropes here. You want to just think your own thoughts, might as well drop out."

"Yeah, I wish," he said.

"Guess what?" she said. "The world's your oyster. You can just drop out and work with your hands and learn how to build hot-air balloons or whatever. Spare the rest of us this nonsense."

"What the fu . . . ? Hot-air balloons?"

"You aren't a child," she said, though he was, though he looked like one. "You like the truth so much?" (I'm not a liar, I'm just kinder than you are, she had told both Tom and Natasha, who thought she was soft just because she was pretty, because she was blond.) "You want me to tell you the truth? If no one else will?" He's a cheater, she thought, but he's also a child.

"Lay it on me," he said.

It would feel good to punch a person in the face. Sometimes it would. "Everybody is putting up with you. You think you're a renegade surrounded by phonies, but those phonies are just being kind. Wearing a fucking top hat."

Now she felt breathless, as though she had run into him and beat at his chest with her fists. She laid her hands palm down flat on the desk to stop their trembling. Out of the corner of her eye she could see that her phone was flashing with a message, but Steven Vandersteen showed no sign of getting out.

"Whoa, lady, I don't know what your deal is, but—"

"You are supposed to address me as Professor."

He stared at her, eyes banded by shadow below the brim of the hat.

"It's very disrespectful." She thought maybe he'd take the hat off and clutch it to his chest in apology and humility.

"So, what do you want me to do about this essay?" he said.

"You're going to take this home and you are going to rewrite it." He nodded at her. "If you don't want to fail," she said, and he continued to nod. In this case, nodding did a great deal to humanize him. "You think you're such a genius?" She smiled at him. "Okay, then. Prove it."

ABOUT THE CONTRIBUTORS

Shashi Bhat holds an MFA in fiction from Johns Hopkins University. Her stories have appeared in *The Malahat Review*, *PRISM international*, *The New Quarterly*, *Grain*, *The Dalhousie Review*, *Journey Prize Stories 24*, and other publications. She has twice been nominated for the Pushcart Prize and was a finalist for the RBC Bronwen Wallace Award for Emerging Writers. Her debut novel, *The Family Took Shape* (Cormorant, 2013), was a finalist for the Thomas Raddall Atlantic Fiction Award. Shashi is the editor of *EVENT* magazine and teaches creative writing at Douglas College.

Greg Brown is a graduate of the University of North Carolina at Greensboro's MFA program in Creative Writing and Memorial University of Newfoundland's MA in English Literature. He is the recipient of the UBC English Department's Roy Daniells Memorial Essay Prize, and his fiction and essays have appeared in *Paragon*, *Postscript*, *Pulp Literature*, *RS500*, *Tate Street*, and elsewhere. He teaches at the University of Virginia's Young Writers Workshop and at the Creative Writing for Children Society of Vancouver. He lives on Vancouver Island and is presently working on a short story collection.

Alicia Elliott is a Tuscarora writer from Six Nations of the Grand River living in Brantford, Ontario, with her husband and child. Her essay "A Mind Spread Out on the Ground" won Gold at the National Magazine Awards in 2017. Her short story "Unearth" was selected for *Best American Short Stories 2018*. She was the 2017–2018 Geoffrey and Margaret Andrew Fellow at UBC, and was selected by Tanya Talaga as the recipient of the 2018 RBC Taylor Prize Emerging Writer Award. Her book of essays, *A Mind Spread Out on the Ground*, is forthcoming from Doubleday Canada in the spring of 2019.

Liz Harmer was born and raised in Hamilton, Ontario, and currently lives in Southern California. Her essays and stories have appeared in *The New Quarterly*, *The Malahat Review*, *Hazlitt*, *Literary Hub*, *Grain*, *PRISM international*, *This Magazine*, and elsewhere. She won the Constance Rooke Creative Nonfiction Prize in 2013 and a National Magazine Award for Personal Journalism in 2014. Her first novel, *The Amateurs*, was published as a New Face of Fiction title with Knopf Canada in 2018. She's at work on a number of new stories and essays, as well as a second novel.

Philip Huynh's fiction has been published in *EVENT*, *The New Quarterly*, *Prairie Schooner*, and *The Malahat Review*, and has been cited in *Best American Short Stories 2015*. "The Forbidden Purple City" is his second story to appear in *The Journey Prize Stories*. His debut collection of stories—coincidentally entitled *The Forbidden Purple City*—co-won the Asian Canadian Writers' Workshop Emerging Writers Award and will be published by Goose Lane Editions in the spring of 2019. He lives in Richmond, B.C., with his wife and twin daughters.

Jason Jobin grew up on an acreage in a Yukon forest. He did a BA and MFA in writing at the University of Victoria, where he studied fiction and screenwriting, and developed his own course on how to rap. His fiction has won *The Malahat Review*'s Jack Hodgins Founders' Award and has been longlisted for *The Fiddlehead* Prize. For him, writing is a place to show the fallout of people in suddenly new situations, the moments that wake you up and that you think back on when falling asleep. He currently lives and writes in Victoria, and is working on a collection and a novel.

Since retiring from a career in education, **Aviva Dale Martin** has returned to writing stories and creative nonfiction. She also takes advantage of this privileged and unique time in her life for dancing, ocean swimming, and cavorting with her brilliant grandchildren. In addition to the publication of "Barcelona" in *PRISM international*, 2017 saw the appearance of her creative nonfiction story, "Manuela," in the Ouen Press anthology *Journey Through Uncertainty and Other Short Stories*. It also received a commendation in their CFN contest in 2016. Aviva lives with Bob, her partner of fifty-one years, in southern, coastal British Columbia, and is currently working on a collection of short stories and a memoir.

Rowan McCandless is a storyteller, thrift store enthusiast, and chai tea lover, who writes from Manitoba's Treaty 1 territory. In 2017, her lyric essay "A Map of the World" won *Room*'s Creative Nonfiction Contest, and she was longlisted for *PRISM international*'s Creative Nonfiction Contest. She placed second in *Prairie Fire*'s 2016 Fiction Contest and *Room*'s 2015 Fiction Contest. Her work has appeared in *Skin Deep: Race and Culture* magazine and is forthcoming in the anthology

Black Writing Matters: Reflections on Contemporary Canadian Life. She continues to publish short fiction and creative non-fiction, and is at work on a novel.

Sofia Mostaghimi is a fiction writer. Her stories have appeared in anthologies, online journals, and print magazines in Canada, the U.S., and Hong Kong. She is also a fiction editor and high school teacher, working in Toronto, Ontario. Of Iranian and Québécois descent, she was born in Sherbrooke, Quebec, and is currently working on a novel, *Desperada*, which builds on the story that appears in this anthology.

Jess Taylor is a Toronto writer and poet. She founded The Emerging Writers Reading Series in 2012. *Pauls*, her first collection of stories, was published by Book*hug in 2015. The title story from the collection, "Paul," received the Gold for Fiction at the 2013 National Magazine Awards. Jess has also released two chapbooks of poetry, *And Then Everyone: Poems of the West End* (Picture Window Press, 2014) and *Never Stop* (Anstruther Press, 2014). Jess' next collection of stories, *Just Pervs*, will be published by Book*hug in 2019. She's currently working on a novel and continuation of her life poem, *Never Stop*.

Iryn Tushabe was born near Kibale Forest in southwestern Uganda, and currently lives in Regina, Saskatchewan. Her creative nonfiction has appeared in *Briarpatch Magazine* and was longlisted for the CBC Creative Nonfiction Prize. Her short fiction had been anthologized in the *CVC7: Carter V Cooper Short Fiction Anthology Series*. A graduate of the Humber

School for Writers, she's currently completing her debut novel, which is set in contemporary rural and urban Uganda.

Carly Vandergriendt left her hometown in Southern Ontario for Montreal in her early twenties, after stints in New Zealand, India, and Mexico. She recently completed a collection of stories set in Montreal, and is now at work on a novel about an environmental activist-turned-fugitive. Her story "The Crossing" won the *Humber Literary Review*'s Emerging Writers Fiction Contest, and her writing has been published in *Prairie Fire*, *The Fiddlehead*, *The Malahat Review*, *CVC*7, *Room*, and elsewhere. Carly holds an MFA in Creative Writing from UBC and works as an English/ESL teacher.

For more information about the publications that submitted
to this year's competition, The Journey Prize, and *The Journey
Prize Stories*, please visit www.facebook.com/TheJourneyPrize.

CVC Anthology Series is an annual publication from Exile
Editions that presents the shortlist and winners from the
$15,000 Carter V. Cooper Short Fiction Competition, which
is open to all Canadian writers, with two prizes awarded:
$10,000 for the best story by an emerging writer, and $5,000
for the best story by a writer at any point of her/his career.
The CVC competition runs November through June, is
administered by *Exile Quarterly* (a literary/visual arts magazine that has also had writers selected to appear in the Journey
Prize anthology, including one winner), and is sponsored by
U.S. philanthropist Gloria Vanderbilt, who awards the prizes
in memory of her son Carter V. Cooper (the deceased brother
of CNN's Anderson Cooper). Website: ExileEditions.com

The Dalhousie Review is an award-winning literary journal
published triannually by Dalhousie University. Now in its
ninety-eighth year, it features poetry, fiction, essays, and interviews by both established and emerging writers in Canada
and from around the world as well as reviews of recent books,
films, albums, and performances. Past contributors include
some of Canada's most celebrated writers, such as Margaret
Atwood, Alfred Bailey, Earle Birney, Elizabeth Brewster,
Charles Bruce, George Elliott Clarke, Fred Cogswell, Laurence

Dakin, Leo Kennedy, A.M. Klein, Kenneth Leslie, Malcolm Lowry, Hugh MacLennan, Alistair MacLeod, Alden Nowlan, A. J. M. Smith, Alice Mackenzie Swaim, W.D. Valgardson, Guy Vanderhaeghe, and Miriam Waddington. Editor: Anthony Enns. Production Manager: Lynne Evans. Correspondence: *The Dalhousie Review*, c/o Dalhousie University, Halifax, Nova Scotia, B3H 4R2. For subscription and submission guidelines, please contact the Production Manager at Dalhousie. Review@dal.ca or visit our website at dalhousiereview.dal.ca.

EVENT has inspired and nurtured writers for almost five decades. Featuring the very best in contemporary writing from Canada and abroad, *EVENT* consistently publishes award-winning fiction, poetry, nonfiction, notes on writing, and critical reviews—all topped off by stunning Canadian cover art and illustrations. Stories first published in *EVENT* regularly appear in the *Best Canadian Stories* and *Journey Prize Stories* anthologies, are finalists at the National Magazine Awards, and recently won the Grand Prix Best Literature and Art Story at the 2017 Canadian Magazine Awards. *EVENT* is also home to Canada's longest-running nonfiction contest (fall deadline), and its Reading Service for Writers. Editor: Shashi Bhat. Managing Editor: Ian Cockfield. Fiction Editor: Christine Dewar. Correspondence: *EVENT*, P.O. Box 2503, New Westminster, British Columbia, V3L 5B2. Email (queries only): event@ douglascollege.ca Website: www.eventmagazine.ca

The Malahat Review is a quarterly journal of contemporary poetry, fiction, and creative nonfiction by both new and celebrated writers. Summer issues feature the winners of *Malahat*'s

Novella and Long Poem prizes, held in alternate years; the fall issues feature the winners of the Far Horizons Award for emerging writers, alternating between poetry and fiction each year; the winter issues feature the winners of the Constance Rooke Creative Nonfiction Prize; and the spring issues feature winners of the Open Season Awards in all three genres (poetry, fiction, and creative nonfiction). All issues feature covers by noted Canadian visual artists and include reviews of Canadian books. Interim Editor: Micaela Maftei. Assistant Editor: Rhonda Batchelor. Correspondence: *The Malahat Review*, University of Victoria, P.O. Box 1700, Station CSC, Victoria, British Columbia, V8W 2Y2. Unsolicited submissions are accepted through Submittable only; contest entries, by email (review contest guidelines before entering). E-mail: malahat@uvic.ca Website: www.malahatreview.ca Twitter: @malahatreview

The New Quarterly is an award-winning literary magazine publishing fiction, poetry, personal essays, interviews, and essays on writing. Founded in 1981, the magazine prides itself on its independent take on the Canadian literary scene. Recent issues include a celebration of diverse voices and one guest-edited by Anna Ling Kaye, with more exciting projects in the works. Editor: Pamela Mulloy. Submissions and correspondence: *The New Quarterly*, c/o St. Jerome's University, 290 Westmount Road North, Waterloo, Ontario, N2L 3G3. E-mail: pmulloy@tnq.ca, sblom@tnq.ca Website: www.tnq.ca

Prairie Fire is an award-winning literary magazine that publishes poetry and prose by emerging and established writers.

Our summer issue features the winners of our annual poetry, fiction, and creative nonfiction contests. In celebration of our fortieth anniversary, the 2018 summer issue will also include new work by writers published in *Prairie Fire*'s formative years, such as Sandra Birdsell and Margaret Sweatman, along with a section featuring Winnipeg writers never before published in *PF*. This fall, *Prairie Fire* is publishing a joint issue with *Contemporary Verse 2*, edited by Warren Cariou and Katherena Vermette, which will highlight Indigenous writers from across the country. Our winter issue includes the Anne Szumigalski Memorial Lecture, which will be delivered this year by Alice Major. Fiction Editors: Lindsey Childs, Melissa Steele, and Andris Taskans. Submissions, correspondence, and contest entries: *Prairie Fire*, 423–100 Arthur Street, Winnipeg, Manitoba, R3B 1H3. Email: prfire@mymts.net Website: www.prairiefire.ca Facebook: @PrairieFireMagazine Twitter: @PrairieFireMag Instagram: @prairiefiremag

PRISM international, the oldest literary magazine in Western Canada, was established in 1959 by Earle Birney at the University of British Columbia. Published four times a year, *PRISM* features short fiction, poetry, creative non-fiction, drama, hybrid forms, and translations. *PRISM* editors select work based on originality and quality, and the magazine showcases work from both new and established writers from Canada and around the world. *PRISM* holds four exemplary annual competitions for short fiction, literary nonfiction, very short forms, and poetry, and awards the Earle Birney Prize for Poetry to an outstanding poet whose work was featured in *PRISM* in the preceding year. Executive Editors: Selina Boan and Jessica Johns. Prose Editor: Kyla Jamieson. Poetry Editor: Shazia Hafiz Ramji. Submissions and correspondence: *PRISM international*, Creative Writing Program, The University of British Columbia, Buchanan E-462, 1866 Main Mall, Vancouver, British Columbia, V6T 1Z1. Website: www.prismmagazine.ca

PULP Literature is a Canadian multi-genre fiction magazine, printing a spectrum of high-end yet accessible stories and poetry, including fantasy, mystery, science fiction, literary, humour, novel excerpts, and short comics. Launched in 2013 through a Kickstarter campaign, the quarterly magazine prides itself on community involvement in the BC Lower Mainland. The press runs four annual literary contests for short fiction and poetry: The Bumblebee Flash Fiction Contest, The Magpie Award for Poetry, The Hummingbird Flash Fiction Prize, and the Raven Short Story Contest. Founding Editors: Jennifer Landels, Susan Pieters, and Mel Anastasiou. Email: info@pulpliterature.com Website: www.pulpliterature.com

For more than five decades, **This Magazine** has proudly published fiction and poetry from new and emerging Canadian writers. A sassy and thoughtful journal of arts, politics, and progressive ideas, *This* consistently offers fresh takes on familiar issues, as well as breaking stories that need to be told. Publisher: Lisa Whittington-Hill. Fiction Editor: Andrew Battershill. Submissions and correspondence: *This Magazine*, Suite 417, 401 Richmond Street West, Toronto, Ontario, M5V 3A8. Website: www.this.org

Submissions were also received from the following publications:

Agnes and True
(Toronto, ON)
www.agnesandtrue.com

Breaking Boundaries:
LGBTQ2 Writers on Coming
Out and Into Canada
www.rebelmountainpress.com

carte blanche
(Montreal, QC)
www.carte-blanche.org

CNQ: Canadian Notes &
Queries
(Windsor, ON)
www.notesandqueries.ca

Cosmonauts Avenue
(Quebec City, QC)
www.cosmonautsavenue.com

The Danforth Review
(Toronto, ON)
www.danforthreview.com

Don't Talk to Me About Love
(Toronto, ON)
www.donttalktomeabout
love.org

The Double World
(Toronto, ON)
www.inkwellworkshops.com

The Fiddlehead
(Fredericton, NB)
www.thefiddlehead.ca

FreeFall
(Calgary, AB)
www.freefallmagazine.ca

Glass Buffalo
(Edmonton, AB)
www.glassbuffalo.com

Grain
(Saskatoon, SK)
www.grainmagazine.ca

The Humber Literary Review
(Toronto, ON)
www.humberliteraryreview.
com

Joyland Magazine
www.joylandmagazine.com

Little Fiction | Big Truths
(Toronto, ON)
www.littlefiction.com

Looseleaf Magazine
(Toronto, ON)
www.looseleafmagazine.ca

Maisonneuve
(Montreal, QC)
www.maisonneuve.org

*Maple Tree Literary
Supplement*
(Montreal, QC)
www.mtls.ca

The New Orphic Review
(Nelson, BC)

On Spec
(Edmonton, AB)
www.onspec.ca

Plenitude Magazine
(Victoria, BC)
www.plenitudemagazine.ca

Prairie Fire
(Winnipeg, MB)
www.prairiefire.ca

The Prairie Journal
(Calgary, AB)
www.prairiejournal.org

The Puritan
(Toronto, ON)
www.puritanmagazine.com

Queen's Quarterly
(Kingston, ON)
www.queensu.ca/quarterly

Ricepaper Magazine
(Vancouver, BC)
www.ricepapermagazine.ca

Riddle Fence
(St. John's, NL)
www.riddlefence.com

Room Magazine
(Vancouver, BC)
www.roommagazine.com

The Rusty Toque
(London, ON)
www.therustytoque.com

subTerrain Magazine
(Vancouver, BC)
www.subterrain.ca

The Walrus
(Toronto, ON)
www.thewalrus.ca

Taddle Creek
(Toronto, ON)
www.taddlecreekmag.com

untethered
(Toronto, ON)
www.alwaysuntethered.com

PREVIOUS CONTRIBUTING AUTHORS

* Winners of the $10,000 Journey Prize
** Co-winners of the $10,000 Journey Prize

1

1989
SELECTED WITH ALISTAIR MacLEOD

Ven Begamudré, "Word Games"

David Bergen, "Where You're From"

Lois Braun, "The Pumpkin-Eaters"

Constance Buchanan, "Man with Flying Genitals"

Ann Copeland, "Obedience"

Marion Douglas, "Flags"

Frances Itani, "An Evening in the Café"

Diane Keating, "The Crying Out"

Thomas King, "One Good Story, That One"

Holley Rubinsky, "Rapid Transits"*

Jean Rysstad, "Winter Baby"

Kevin Van Tighem, "Whoopers"

M.G. Vassanji, "In the Quiet of a Sunday Afternoon"

Bronwen Wallace, "Chicken 'N' Ribs"

Armin Wiebe, "Mouse Lake"

Budge Wilson, "Waiting"

2

1990
SELECTED WITH LEON ROOKE; GUY VANDERHAEGHE

André Alexis, "Despair: Five Stories of Ottawa"

Glen Allen, "The Hua Guofeng Memorial Warehouse"

Marusia Bociurkiw, "Mama, Donya"

Virgil Burnett, "Billfrith the Dreamer"

Margaret Dyment, "Sacred Trust"

Cynthia Flood, "My Father Took a Cake to France"*

Douglas Glover, "Story Carved in Stone"

Terry Griggs, "Man with the Axe"

Rick Hillis, "Limbo River"

Thomas King, "The Dog I Wish I Had, I Would Call It Helen"
K.D. Miller, "Sunrise Till Dark"
Jennifer Mitton, "Let Them Say"
Lawrence O'Toole, "Goin' to Town with Katie Ann"
Kenneth Radu, "A Change of Heart"
Jenifer Sutherland, "Table Talk"
Wayne Tefs, "Red Rock and After"

3
1991
SELECTED WITH JANE URQUHART

Donald Aker, "The Invitation"
Anton Baer, "Yukon"
Allan Barr, "A Visit from Lloyd"
David Bergen, "The Fall"
Rai Berzins, "Common Sense"
Diana Hartog, "Theories of Grief"
Diane Keating, "The Salem Letters"
Yann Martel, "The Facts Behind the Helsinki Roccamatios"*
Jennifer Mitton, "Polaroid"
Sheldon Oberman, "This Business with Elijah"
Lynn Podgurny, "Till Tomorrow, Maple Leaf Mills"
James Riseborough, "She Is Not His Mother"
Patricia Stone, "Living on the Lake"

4
1992
SELECTED WITH SANDRA BIRDSELL

David Bergen, "The Bottom of the Glass"
Maria A. Billion, "No Miracles Sweet Jesus"
Judith Cowan, "By the Big River"
Steven Heighton, "How Beautiful upon the Mountains"
Steven Heighton, "A Man Away from Home Has No Neighbours"
L. Rex Kay, "Travelling"
Rozena Maart, "No Rosa, No District Six"*
Guy Malet De Carteret, "Rainy Day"
Carmelita McGrath, "Silence"
Michael Mirolla, "A Theory of Discontinuous Existence"
Diane Juttner Perreault, "Bella's Story"
Eden Robinson, "Traplines"

5

1993

SELECTED WITH GUY VANDERHAEGHE

Caroline Adderson, "Oil and Dread"

David Bergen, "La Rue Prevette"

Marina Endicott, "With the Band"

Dayv James-French, "Cervine"

Michael Kenyon, "Durable Tumblers"

K.D. Miller, "A Litany in Time of Plague"

Robert Mullen, "Flotsam"

Gayla Reid, "Sister Doyle's Men"*

Oakland Ross, "Bang-bang"

Robert Sherrin, "Technical Battle for Trial Machine"

Carol Windley, "The Etruscans"

6

1994

SELECTED WITH DOUGLAS GLOVER;
JUDITH CHANT (CHAPTERS)

Anne Carson, "Water Margins: An Essay on Swimming by My Brother"

Richard Cumyn, "The Sound He Made"

Genni Gunn, "Versions"

Melissa Hardy, "Long Man the River"*

Robert Mullen, "Anomie"

Vivian Payne, "Free Falls"

Jim Reil, "Dry"

Robyn Sarah, "Accept My Story"

Joan Skogan, "Landfall"

Dorothy Speak, "Relatives in Florida"

Alison Wearing, "Notes from Under Water"

7

1995

SELECTED WITH M.G. VASSANJI;
RICHARD BACHMANN (A DIFFERENT DRUMMER BOOKS)

Michelle Alfano, "Opera"

Mary Borsky, "Maps of the Known World"

Gabriella Goliger, "Song of Ascent"

Elizabeth Hay, "Hand Games"

Shaena Lambert, "The Falling Woman"

Elise Levine, "Boy"

Roger Burford Mason, "The Rat-Catcher's Kiss"
Antanas Sileika, "Going Native"
Kathryn Woodward, "Of Marranos and Gilded Angels"*

8
1996
SELECTED WITH OLIVE SENIOR;
BEN MCNALLY (NICHOLAS HOARE LTD.)

Rick Bowers, "Dental Bytes"
David Elias, "How I Crossed Over"
Elyse Gasco, "Can You Wave Bye Bye, Baby?"*
Danuta Gleed, "Bones"
Elizabeth Hay, "The Friend"
Linda Holeman, "Turning the Worm"
Elaine Littman, "The Winner's Circle"
Murray Logan, "Steam"
Rick Maddocks, "Lessons from the Sputnik Diner"
K.D. Miller, "Egypt Land"
Gregor Robinson, "Monster Gaps"
Alma Subasic, "Dust"

9
1997
SELECTED WITH NINO RICCI; NICHOLAS PASHLEY
(UNIVERSITY OF TORONTO BOOKSTORE)

Brian Bartlett, "Thomas, Naked"
Dennis Bock, "Olympia"
Kristen den Hartog, "Wave"
Gabriella Goliger, "Maladies of the Inner Ear"**
Terry Griggs, "Momma Had a Baby"
Mark Anthony Jarman, "Righteous Speedboat"
Judith Kalman, "Not for Me a Crown of Thorns"
Andrew Mullins, "The World of Science"
Sasenarine Persaud, "Canada Geese and Apple Chatney"
Anne Simpson, "Dreaming Snow"**
Sarah Withrow, "Ollie"
Terence Young, "The Berlin Wall"

10
1998
SELECTED BY PETER BUITENHUIS; HOLLEY RUBINSKY; CELIA DUTHIE (DUTHIE BOOKS LTD.)

John Brooke, "The Finer Points of Apples"*
Ian Colford, "The Reason for the Dream"
Libby Creelman, "Cruelty"
Michael Crummey, "Serendipity"
Stephen Guppy, "Downwind"
Jane Eaton Hamilton, "Graduation"
Elise Levine, "You Are You Because Your Little Dog Loves You"
Jean McNeil, "Bethlehem"
Liz Moore, "Eight-Day Clock"
Edward O'Connor, "The Beatrice of Victoria College"
Tim Rogers, "Scars and Other Presents"
Denise Ryan, "Marginals, Vivisections, and Dreams"
Madeleine Thien, "Simple Recipes"
Cheryl Tibbetts, "Flowers of Africville"

11
1999
SELECTED BY LESLEY CHOYCE; SHELDON CURRIE; MARY-JO ANDERSON (FROG HOLLOW BOOKS)

Mike Barnes, "In Florida"
Libby Creelman, "Sunken Island"
Mike Finigan, "Passion Sunday"
Jane Eaton Hamilton, "Territory"
Mark Anthony Jarman, "Travels into Several Remote Nations of the
   World"
Barbara Lambert, "Where the Bodies Are Kept"
Linda Little, "The Still"
Larry Lynch, "The Sitter"
Sandra Sabatini, "The One With the News"
Sharon Steams, "Brothers"
Mary Walters, "Show Jumping"
Alissa York, "The Back of the Bear's Mouth"*

12

2000

SELECTED BY CATHERINE BUSH; HAL NIEDZVIECKI; MARC GLASSMAN (PAGES BOOKS AND MAGAZINES)

Andrew Gray, "The Heart of the Land"

Lee Henderson, "Sheep Dub"

Jessica Johnson, "We Move Slowly"

John Lavery, "The Premier's New Pyjamas"

J.A. McCormack, "Hearsay"

Nancy Richler, "Your Mouth Is Lovely"

Andrew Smith, "Sightseeing"

Karen Solie, "Onion Calendar"

Timothy Taylor, "Doves of Townsend"*

Timothy Taylor, "Pope's Own"

Timothy Taylor, "Silent Cruise"

R.M. Vaughan, "Swan Street"

13

2001

SELECTED BY ELYSE GASCO; MICHAEL HELM; MICHAEL NICHOLSON (INDIGO BOOKS & MUSIC INC.)

Kevin Armstrong, "The Cane Field"*

Mike Barnes, "Karaoke Mon Amour"

Heather Birrell, "Machaya"

Heather Birrell, "The Present Perfect"

Craig Boyko, "The Gun"

Vivette J. Kady, "Anything That Wiggles"

Billie Livingston, "You're Taking All the Fun Out of It"

Annabel Lyon, "Fishes"

Lisa Moore, "The Way the Light Is"

Heather O'Neill, "Little Suitcase"

Susan Rendell, "In the Chambers of the Sea"

Tim Rogers, "Watch"

Margrith Schraner, "Dream Dig"

14
2002
SELECTED BY ANDRÉ ALEXIS;
DEREK McCORMACK; DIANE SCHOEMPERLEN

Mike Barnes, "Cogagwee"

Geoffrey Brown, "Listen"

Jocelyn Brown, "Miss Canada"*

Emma Donoghue, "What Remains"

Jonathan Goldstein, "You Are a Spaceman With Your Head Under the
    Bathroom Stall Door"

Robert McGill, "Confidence Men"

Robert McGill, "The Stars Are Falling"

Nick Melling, "Philemon"

Robert Mullen, "Alex the God"

Karen Munro, "The Pool"

Leah Postman, "Being Famous"

Neil Smith, "Green Fluorescent Protein"

15
2003
SELECTED BY MICHELLE BERRY;
TIMOTHY TAYLOR; MICHAEL WINTER

Rosaria Campbell, "Reaching"

Hilary Dean, "The Lemon Stories"

Dawn Rae Downton, "Hansel and Gretel"

Anne Fleming, "Gay Dwarves of America"

Elyse Friedman, "Truth"

Charlotte Gill, "Hush"

Jessica Grant, "My Husband's Jump"*

Jacqueline Honnet, "Conversion Classes"

S.K. Johannesen, "Resurrection"

Avner Mandelman, "Cuckoo"

Tim Mitchell, "Night Finds Us"

Heather O'Neill, "The Difference Between Me and Goldstein"

16

2004

SELECTED BY ELIZABETH HAY; LISA MOORE; MICHAEL REDHILL

Anar Ali, "Baby Khaki's Wings"

Kenneth Bonert, "Packers and Movers"

Jennifer Clouter, "Benny and the Jets"

Daniel Griffin, "Mercedes Buyer's Guide"

Michael Kissinger, "Invest in the North"

Devin Krukoff, "The Last Spark"*

Elaine McCluskey, "The Watermelon Social"

William Metcalfe, "Nice Big Car, Rap Music Coming Out the Window"

Lesley Millard, "The Uses of the Neckerchief"

Adam Lewis Schroeder, "Burning the Cattle at Both Ends"

Michael V. Smith, "What We Wanted"

Neil Smith, "Isolettes"

Patricia Rose Young, "Up the Clyde on a Bike"

17

2005

SELECTED BY JAMES GRAINGER AND NANCY LEE

Randy Boyagoda, "Rice and Curry Yacht Club"

Krista Bridge, "A Matter of Firsts"

Josh Byer, "Rats, Homosex, Saunas, and Simon"

Craig Davidson, "Failure to Thrive"

McKinley M. Hellenes, "Brighter Thread"

Catherine Kidd, "Green-Eyed Beans"

Pasha Malla, "The Past Composed"

Edward O'Connor, "Heard Melodies Are Sweet"

Barbara Romanik, "Seven Ways into Chandigarh"

Sandra Sabatini, "The Dolphins at Sainte Marie"

Matt Shaw, "Matchbook for a Mother's Hair"*

Richard Simas, "Anthropologies"

Neil Smith, "Scrapbook"

Emily White, "Various Metals"

18
2006
SELECTED BY STEVEN GALLOWAY;
ZSUZSI GARTNER; ANNABEL LYON

Heather Birrell, "BriannaSusannaAlana"*
Craig Boyko, "The Baby"
Craig Boyko, "The Beloved Departed"
Nadia Bozak, "Heavy Metal Housekeeping"
Lee Henderson, "Conjugation"
Melanie Little, "Wrestling"
Matthew Rader, "The Lonesome Death of Joseph Fey"
Scott Randall, "Law School"
Sarah Selecky, "Throwing Cotton"
Damian Tarnopolsky, "Sleepy"
Martin West, "Cretacea"
David Whitton, "The Eclipse"
Clea Young, "Split"

19
2007
SELECTED BY CAROLINE ADDERSON;
DAVID BEZMOZGIS; DIONNE BRAND

Andrew J. Borkowski, "Twelve Versions of Lech"
Craig Boyko, "OZY"*
Grant Buday, "The Curve of the Earth"
Nicole Dixon, "High-Water Mark"
Krista Foss, "Swimming in Zanzibar"
Pasha Malla, "Respite"
Alice Petersen, "After Summer"
Patricia Robertson, "My Hungarian Sister"
Rebecca Rosenblum, "Chilly Girl"
Nicholas Ruddock, "How Eunice Got Her Baby"
Jean Van Loon, "Stardust"

20
2008
SELECTED BY LYNN COADY; HEATHER O'NEILL; NEIL SMITH

Théodora Armstrong, "Whale Stories"

Mike Christie, "Goodbye Porkpie Hat"

Anna Leventhal, "The Polar Bear at the Museum"

Naomi K. Lewis, "The Guiding Light"

Oscar Martens, "Breaking on the Wheel"

Dana Mills, "Steaming for Godthab"

Saleema Nawaz, "My Three Girls"*

Scott Randall, "The Gifted Class"

S. Kennedy Sobol, "Some Light Down"

Sarah Steinberg, "At Last at Sea"

Clea Young, "Chaperone"

21
2009
SELECTED BY CAMILLA GIBB;
LEE HENDERSON; REBECCA ROSENBLUM

Daniel Griffin, "The Last Great Works of Alvin Cale"

Jesus Hardwell, "Easy Living"

Paul Headrick, "Highlife"

Sarah Keevil, "Pyro"

Adrian Michael Kelly, "Lure"

Fran Kimmel, "Picturing God's Ocean"

Lynne Kutsukake, "Away"

Alexander MacLeod, "Miracle Mile"

Dave Margoshes, "The Wisdom of Solomon"

Shawn Syms, "On the Line"

Sarah L. Taggart, "Deaf"

Yasuko Thanh, "Floating Like the Dead"*

22
2010
SELECTED BY PASHA MALLA; JOAN THOMAS; ALISSA YORK

Carolyn Black, "Serial Love"

Andrew Boden, "Confluence of Spoors"

Laura Boudreau, "The Dead Dad Game"

Devon Code, "Uncle Oscar"*

Danielle Egan, "Publicity"

Krista Foss, "The Longitude of Okay"

Lynne Kutsukake, "Mating"

Ben Lof, "When in the Field with Her at His Back"

Andrew MacDonald, "Eat Fist!"

Eliza Robertson, "Ship's Log"

Mike Spry, "Five Pounds Short and Apologies to Nelson Algren"

Damian Tarnopolsky, "Laud We the Gods"

23
2011
SELECTED BY ALEXANDER MACLEOD;
ALISON PICK; SARAH SELECKY

Jay Brown, "The Girl from the War"

Michael Christie, "The Extra"

Seyward Goodhand, "The Fur Trader's Daughter"

Miranda Hill, "Petitions to Saint Chronic"*

Fran Kimmel, "Laundry Day"

Ross Klatte, "First-Calf Heifer"

Michelle Serwatuk, "My Eyes Are Dim"

Jessica Westhead, "What I Would Say"

Michelle Winters, "Toupée"

D.W. Wilson, "The Dead Roads"

24
2012
SELECTED BY MICHAEL CHRISTIE;
KATHRYN KUITENBROUWER; KATHLEEN WINTER

Kris Bertin, "Is Alive and Can Move"
Shashi Bhat, "Why I Read *Beowulf*"
Astrid Blodgett, "Ice Break"
Trevor Corkum, "You Were Loved"
Nancy Jo Cullen, "Ashes"
Kevin Hardcastle, "To Have to Wait"
Andrew Hood, "I'm Sorry and Thank You"
Andrew Hood, "Manning"
Grace O'Connell, "The Many Faces of Montgomery Clift"
Jasmina Odor, "Barcelona"
Alex Pugsley, "Crisis on Earth-X"*
Eliza Robertson, "Sea Drift"
Martin West, "My Daughter of the Dead Reeds"

25
2013
SELECTED BY MIRANDA HILL;
MARK MEDLEY; RUSSELL WANGERSKY

Steven Benstead, "Megan's Bus"
Jay Brown, "The Egyptians"
Andrew Forbes, "In the Foothills"
Philip Huynh, "Gulliver's Wife"
Amy Jones, "Team Ninja"
Marnie Lamb, "Mrs. Fujimoto's Wednesday Afternoons"
Doretta Lau, "How Does a Single Blade of Grass Thank the Sun?"
Laura Legge, "It's Raining in Paris"
Natalie Morrill, "Ossicles"
Zoey Leigh Peterson, "Sleep World"
Eliza Robertson, "My Sister Sang"
Naben Ruthnum, "Cinema Rex"*

26
2014
SELECTED BY STEVEN W. BEATTIE;
CRAIG DAVIDSON; SALEEMA NAWAZ

Rosaria Campbell, "Probabilities"
Nancy Jo Cullen, "Hashtag Maggie Vandermeer"
M.A. Fox, "Piano Boy"
Kevin Hardcastle, "Old Man Marchuk"
Amy Jones, "Wolves, Cigarettes, Gum"
Tyler Keevil, "Sealskin"*
Jeremy Lanaway, "Downturn"
Andrew MacDonald, "Four Minutes"
Lori McNulty, "Monsoon Season"
Shana Myara, "Remainders"
Julie Roorda, "How to Tell if Your Frog Is Dead"
Leona Theis, "High Beams"
Clea Young, "Juvenile"

27
2015
SELECTED BY ANTONY DE SA,
TANIS RIDEOUT, AND CARRIE SNYDER

Charlotte Bondy, "Renaude"
Emily Bossé, "Last Animal Standing on Gentleman's Farm"
Deirdre Dore, "The Wise Baby"*
Charlie Fiset, "Maggie's Farm"
K'ari Fisher, "Mercy Beatrice Wrestles the Noose"
Anna Ling Kaye, "Red Egg and Ginger"
Andrew MacDonald, "The Perfect Man for my Husband"
Madeleine Maillet, "Achilles' Death"
Lori McNulty, "Fingernecklace"
Sarah Meehan Sirk, "Moonman"
Ron Schafrick, "Lovely Company"
Georgia Wilder, "Cocoa Divine and the Lightning Police"

28

2016

SELECTED BY KATE CAYLEY;
BRIAN FRANCIS; MADELEINE THIEN

Carleigh Baker, "Chins and Elbows"

Paige Cooper, "The Roar"

Charlie Fiset, "If I Ever See the Sun"

Mahak Jain, "The Origin of Jaanvi"

Colette Langlois, "The Emigrants"*

Alex Leslie, "The Person You Want to See"

Andrew MacDonald, "Progress on a Genetic Level"

J.R. McConvey, "Home Range"

J.R. McConvey, "How the Grizzly Came to Hang in the Royal Oak Hotel"

Souvankham Thammavongsa, "Mani Pedi"

Souvankham Thammavongsa, "Paris"

29

2017

SELECTED BY KEVIN HARDCASTLE;
GRACE O'CONNELL; AYELET TSABARI

Lisa Alward, "Old Growth"

Sharon Bala, "Butter Tea at Starbucks"*

Sharon Bala, "Reading Week"

Patrick Doerksen, "Leech"

Sarah Kabamba, "They Come Crying

Michael Meagher, "Used to It"

Darlene Naponse, "She Is Water"

Maria Reva, "Subject Winifred"

Jack Wang, "The Nature of Things"

Kelly Ward, "A Girl and a Dog on a Friday Night"